MASADA

The Last Fortress

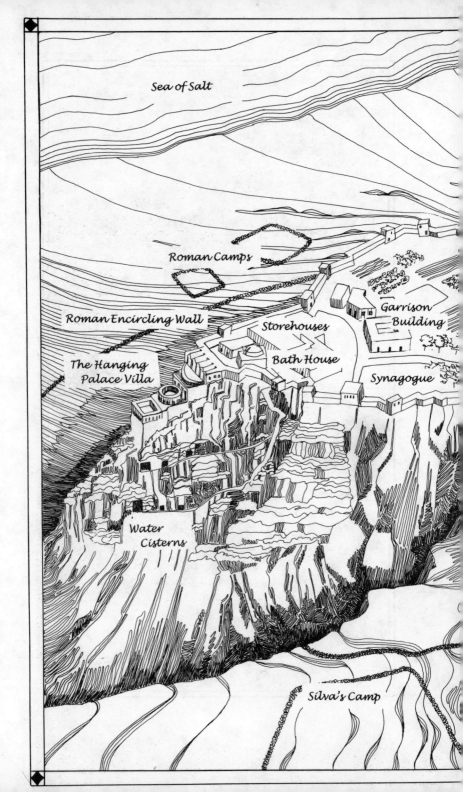

Roman
Overlooking
Camp

Underground
Cistern

Southern
Bastion

Western
Palace

Bathing Pool

The Ram Tower

Ramp

Roman Encircling Wall

Roman Camp

MASADA

MASADA
The Last Fortress

Gloria D. Miklowitz

EERDMANS BOOKS FOR YOUNG READERS
GRAND RAPIDS, MICHIGAN / CAMBRIDGE, U.K.

© 1998 Gloria D. Miklowitz

Published 1998 by
Eerdmans Books for Young Readers
an imprint of
Wm. B. Eerdmans Publishing Co.
255 Jefferson Ave. S.E., Grand Rapids, Michigan 49503 /
P.O. Box 163, Cambridge CB3 9PU U.K.

Paperback edition 1999

Printed in the United States of America

03 02 01 00 99   7 6 5 4 3 2

Library of Congress Cataloging-in-Publication Data

Miklowitz, Gloria D.
Masada: the last fortress / written by Gloria Miklowitz.
p.   cm.
Summary: As the Roman army marches inexorably across the Judean desert
toward the fortress of Masada, Simon and his family and friends prepare,
along with the rest of the Jewish Zealots, to fight and never surrender.
ISBN 0-8028-5168-1 (pbk: alk. paper).
1. Masada Site (Israel) — Siege, 72-73 — Juvenile fiction.
[1. Masada Site (Israel) — Siege, 72-73 — Fiction.
2. Jews — History — Rebellion, 66-73 — Fiction.]
I. Title.
PZ7.M593Mas   1998
[Fic] — dc21   98-17756
CIP
AC

In memory of my dear husband, Julius,
who made this book possible

Acknowledgments

I owe much gratitude to Mary Hietbrink, my wonderful editor, for her enthusiasm, help, and unflagging patience. And I owe many thanks to my friend and colleague Tony Johnston, who read the manuscript with a poet's eye and offered a great many valuable suggestions.

About the Story

In 72 C.E., in the country of Judea, now called Israel, 960 Jews lived on a mountain fortress called Masada, near the Dead Sea. It had been built a hundred years before by King Herod, and had vast water supplies, storerooms full of food and weapons, and two magnificent palaces. Rising twelve hundred feet above the desert floor, it seemed impossible to assault.

Many of the Jews on Masada had escaped to the fortress when Jerusalem, their spiritual capital, fell to the Romans in 70 C.E., after four years of a bitter and bloody war. Though the war had officially ended, with many thousands of their people killed, these Zealots remained free. From their safe mountaintop they made frequent attacks on Roman-held towns nearby, a situation the Romans would not tolerate.

Vespasian, Roman emperor at that time, ordered Flavius Silva, commander of the famous Roman Tenth Legion, to subdue these rebellious troublemakers and take Masada. Those who resisted should be killed, he said, and the rest brought back to Rome as slaves.

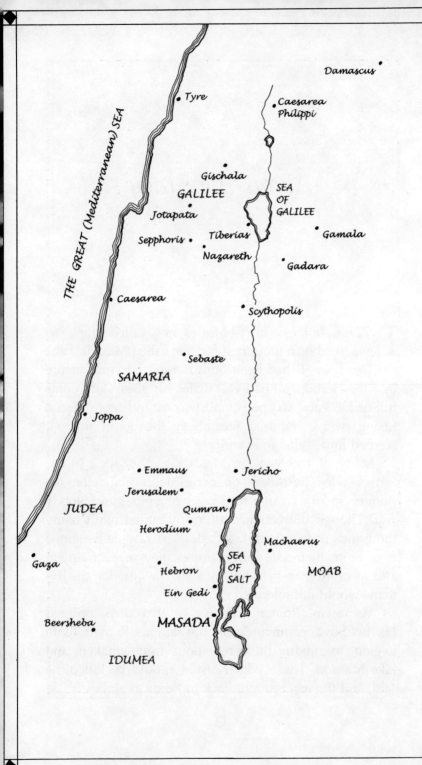

MASADA

The Last Fortress

Chapter I

I, Simon, son of Eleazar ben Ya'ir, begin this journal in the Hebrew year 3833, the month of Elul, writing of our life and hopes here at Masada in the kingdom of Judea. I begin with peace and gladness in my heart, for it is now near three years that we have been living here, and as yet the Romans do not come.

Every day, when we are not working our small fields, or studying in the synagogue classroom, or fashioning weapons under my father's guidance, we are on the casemate wall — John, Deborah, and myself. We shield our eyes against the glaring sun and look eastward to the Sea of Salt and the mountains of Moab; or to the south along the sandy shore; or the north, toward Ein Gedi and Jerusalem beyond; or the west, toward the nearby hills.

"Surely they will not come here," insists my friend John. "Of what importance is another thousand Jews to the mighty Romans?"

I think his words over carefully and want to believe that he is right, for I have other ambitions for my life than to live as a soldier. Then I look at Deborah, her long, shiny

3

hair whipped against her face by the hot winds that sear the crops in this season. Her almond-shaped eyes are dark with fears and experiences she will not speak about. And I remember how it was in Jotapata, and in Jerusalem before we fled.

"Look," John says. And he throws a stone over the casemate wall so that it falls and tumbles along the steep slopes of our fortress to the desert floor below. "The snake path on the eastern slope is the only road to this fortress. Neither mountain goat nor Roman would try its narrow, twisting way!"

"But, to the west?" Deborah asks, hoping, I think, to have her fears allayed.

Yes, the west. It is the west that haunts me too, for there lies a bridge of land some 300 cubits below our walls that crosses to another hill. And though it seems impossible that any force could attack us from such a place, I would rather that Masada stood as an island in this desert. I know too that Masada was taken once before, by our own people, though the Roman garrison holding it then was small and easily overcome.

But the Romans are determined and well organized now, and if they should wish to scale a wall, even our steep cliffs, they would find a way. I cannot deepen the fear in Deborah's eyes, so I say with a false smile of confidence, "Impossible! With nearly 350 cubits of stone wall to assault? And how could they survive without food or water below? There is no spring within many miles of Masada. Think how far they would have to travel to bring the necessaries of life to their camps."

Deborah thinks this over for a while in her quiet, gentle way, then smiles gratefully at me as she offers us a plate of figs. Food and water are plentiful on Masada. This amazed us all when we first arrived. A hundred years and more ago, King Herod had built giant cisterns here, which captured the water from the hard but infrequent rains. These waters could supply us generously for years. The storehouses, stocked first by Herod and later by the Romans garrisoned at this place, are full of wine and oils, corn and pulse, supplying all our needs.

We even found weapons: spears, bows and arrows, swords, knives, and rocks — weapons Herod had stored for his own protection. For it is said he feared that Cleopatra would convince Antony to take Judea for her. And though a Jew, he was not popular with our people. So it is said that Herod equipped Masada as a refuge for himself. And indeed, it seems an impregnable fortress.

John, Deborah, and I often walk around this plateau, our sandals kicking up small clouds of dust. The everydayness of our life lulls fear, and in this moment, perhaps, we all dare dream there will be time to fulfill ambitions, to laugh, to live, to love.

Goats and sheep wander among the children, who play with loud cries of delight as they shoot round pebbles into a circle. Clothes dry flapping like wings in the wind. Women walk gingerly, balancing heavy jugs of water from the nearest cistern on their heads. A class of young boys trips lightly behind the rabbi, imitating his choppy steps as he heads toward the bath house. Like an old song, the chanting prayers of a grandfather seated in the shade of the wall mingle with the hungry cries of a newborn. The cooking fires in our rooms between the walls yield the same smells I remember from our old home to the north.

"If only they had been reasonable" is John's familiar lament. He scoops up a handful of soil, marveling at the richness of it in an area so arid. John is tall and powerfully built, a natural farmer. Were it not for the war, he would have tended his family's land in the Galilee to the end of his days.

"If only they had been less greedy!" Deborah protests, stepping aside as two children nearly run into her. "My father says he did not mind the Roman rule or the crushing taxes as long as they let us worship in our way. But when they defiled our streets with swine and ripped the Torah to shreds before our eyes . . ." She closes her eyes in remembrance, and tears of anger streak her face. Deborah's father had been on the Sanhedrin, the ruling council of Jews. He had voiced the people's protests to Florus, the Roman governor. The delegation, among the most dignified of our people, had been greeted with taunts and scorn and sent away with threats of even greater taxation, even greater restrictions on their religious freedom. And so began our journey, which has ended here.

WAS IT ONLY YESTERDAY that I began this journal? It seems like years.

I shall not easily forget this day. We three met as usual in the shade of Herod's great palace. The structure cascades in three tiers down the north face of the plateau. Its stairs of handhewn stone lead down thirty-one cubits from the first to the second terrace, and another twenty-one from the second to the third, turning round a column in a spiral, and completely hidden from view. The sumptuous rooms of the palace, with their colorfully painted walls and artfully wrought mosaic floors, were built with Jewish taxes, and we feel no guilt at using them for our purposes. Often we scour the terraces for usable weapons. We haul up the narrow stairs provisions we find cached there, or rocks suitable for rolling down on an enemy. Sometimes we find Aram, my brother, and Sara, his sweetheart, sharing a quiet hour. It is clear that they too feel the need for privacy away from the noise and press of a thousand people in too small a place.

On this day of which I write, we were on the lower terrace, for we often had it to ourselves, most people being unwilling to climb down the many stairs in search of privacy. John was at the parapet, tracing patterns with his bare toes on the ground. Deborah was resting on her back, her arms pillowing her head, staring up at the cloudless sky. Aram and Sara whispered together nearby. And I leaned on the stone wall, my face turned to catch the slight breeze. I remember we were talking about the future.

"I will go back to the Galilee when this is over," John said, "and I will plant in the spring, and plow in the summer, and reap in the fall." His eyes held a faraway look, and his fingers moved as though they could feel the soil that his mind's eye could see. "The seasons will bring rain and sun, even frost and snow," he said. "Oh, how I miss the green of our hills! This endless barrenness; this relentless heat . . ."

"And what will you do, Simon?" Deborah asked sleepily.

Before my eyes flashed the agonized faces of those I had seen dying of famine in Jerusalem, and of those whose hands had been cut off by the Romans when they tried to surrender — who had been sent back to Jerusalem as symbols of Roman "mercy." Perhaps I am a coward (though I have fought the Romans hand to hand), because really, I fear combat, and I ache at others' pain. There must come a day when life will be normal again. Then I will help the living.

"Perhaps I will become a doctor," I said, lulled by the peace of the afternoon into believing that all our ambitions would someday be fulfilled. Then I saw it.

7

At first it appeared but a distant dust cloud, perhaps a sudden sandstorm, common for this season of the year, and I watched it idly, for it seemed localized some forty or so furlongs to the north. I remember now no sense of fear. Only vague awareness. My eyes searched the familiar landscape. After a time, the dust seemed thicker.

"I think it is the hamsin," I said. The hot, humid winds of the hamsin have been known to blow for weeks. Whole villages can be covered with sand, almost buried by the driving wind that rearranges the dunes. John turned and looked in the direction I was facing, and Deborah joined us on the parapet. Aram and Sara rose and came to our sides, as though sensing something of moment. Together we watched in silence as the cloud drew closer, and I felt my heart constrict when I recognized what it was. Deborah knew at the same instant, for her hands reached for John's and mine. On the stifling desert air came the dull thud of thousands of feet marching, advancing on Masada.

We looked at each other, mute, hearing the shouts of our people above as they too recognized the Romans' approach. John's face wrinkled with grief, and I could feel tears start at my eyes, tears of anger and despair. Deborah had the look of an injured fawn, but she seemed more controlled than John or I as she embraced each of us in turn, then darted up the steep stairs, upward to our people.

Chapter II

I, Flavius Silva, Governor of the Kingdom of Judea, Commander in Chief of the Roman Tenth Legion, set down these thoughts in private so that the record may be clear. Let it be known that I have served the Empire well, and judge me accordingly.

It is nearly two weeks now since we left Jerusalem, traveling slowly, because of our numbers, through the Judean desert in the hottest month, September, in the third year of Vespasian's reign. We are unwieldy, being twenty thousand strong. Though most of these are bearers, prisoners of war who carry provisions for the coming siege, our real strength lies in our fighting men — veterans of many battles against the Jews, disciplined, in superb physical condition, and with morale high from our recent successes in Jerusalem.

How foolish these Jews to think they could live as free men, to think they could challenge the might of the Roman Empire! They are as flies on a lion, yet persistent flies! Perhaps we underestimated the spirit of these people. For at first, although unschooled in fighting ways, weapon-poor, and disorganized, they fought back with wild, fanatic fury, and though their losses were heavy, their early battles with our forces ended in victory.

Of course this could not be tolerated. If one small kingdom broke free, might not another try? And so it was that Emperor Nero called from retirement the mightiest general of them all, Vespasian, and sent him here to quell this latest insurrection.

Though I am reluctant to admit that the Jews had cause to rebel, I allow that it is so. Florus, the Roman governor for two years here, used his power ruthlessly. He bled these people for their shekels and gold talents to fill his coffers, and for the mere sport of it taunted them to the limits of their patience. Perhaps the fault lies not with him but with the system. If I should by some stroke become Caesar (and what general has not entertained that possibility since Vespasian reached the throne?), I should change the requirements for our provincial governors. For after all, when a man *buys* his position, it is only natural that he should then wish to recoup his payment, and make a handsome profit besides. Such leadership does not lend itself to fairness in governing, I would say, or dedication to the needs of those governed.

It is six years since the rebellion of the Jews began, and only now is the end in sight. The Galilee and some three million people have already been conquered and destroyed by our armies. Jerusalem, the spiritual capital of these people, has fallen, and with it the Temple. I will not relate the details of that conquest here, for that is another story. Only will I say that internal strife, caused by the lawless, undisciplined element who gained control in Jerusalem, is as much to thank for that victory as the proficiency of our troops. It is rumored that under siege the city was torn by opposing factions, utterly destroyed in morals and spirit, and starved to desperation.

But I digress.

Picture us now, as we move along the desert floor like a gigantic serpent curving its way surely and relentlessly toward its prey, Masada.

Like a great reptilian body, our forces measure three miles, more or less. Our vanguard, the light-armed auxiliaries and bowmen, are like the serpent's head, poised to strike at any sudden enemy attack, protecting the main body from ambushes. Behind them come the heavy-armed troops, both mounted and on foot, followed by ten men from every century carrying their own kits and the instruments for marking out the campsite. Then come the men who straighten out bends in the roadway along which we move, cut paths through the woods, and level rough surfaces so that our army which follows will not become exhausted by marching.

A strong cavalry force protects the men bearing my personal baggage and that of my six military tribunes and sixty centurions.

Behind this, I ride, surrounded by the cream of my cavalry and infantry and a body of expert spear-throwers. The 120 cavalry of the legion follows us, and is backed up by mules carrying battering rams and other mechanical devices. Next come my generals, cohort commanders, and tribunes, with a bodyguard of picked troops; bearers carrying our standards — the Roman eagle; the trumpeters; and last, the main body of men, shoulder to shoulder, six abreast.

These are but half of our numbers — even less — for now trudge thousands of Jewish prisoners of war who carry the food, lumber, and water supplies for the legion, and look after the soldiers' baggage. And after them,

11

thousands more, the mercenaries, protected by a rear-guard of light and heavy infantry and a strong body of cavalry.

Impressive? Certainly. Enough to terrify any enemy even before the first arrow is shot.

I must speculate, now, on the enemy, for as we draw nearer to the rock they call Masada, their nature fills my mind with wonder, and even a reluctant admiration. Not all feel as I. Marius, my second in command, scorns them so deeply it is like a sickness that eats at his reason. But determine for yourself. For some might say that envy of his youth and courage clouds my judgment.

Imagine him with me now as I relate the scene between us earlier in this day.

The sun is bright, the heat heavy. No longer do sudden visions of water in the distance stir comment, for by now we know them to be tricks of light. Marius rides beside me for a time, but when the Sea of Salt comes in view at last, his lips twitch with smiles that start and vanish, and his eyes burn with too bright a light. Finally, he can wait no longer.

He takes his leave and rides ahead to join the vanguard, hoping, I believe, to get the first glimpse of the enemy he hungers to engage. A solid man of compact build, he gallops back and forth, searching the hills for the characteristic stronghold, for we wind our way along the Sea of Salt now, and the rock must not be far.

I see him now, spurring toward me with triumph in his restless eyes, sweating from the awful heat, dusty from the hellish sands of this devil's land twelve hundred feet below the sea. A man so eager for battle might be an asset to any army. But he is one to watch, for hate, not reason, rules him.

"The rock they call Masada is ahead!" he says, the

words coming in gasps from the ride. He guides his horse to fall in line with mine. I look ahead, embarrassed by his uncontrolled passion, scornful of this war-lust.

"It is just as Josephus described, Flavius," he whispers hoarsely, his voice still fighting for control. "The palace of Herod hangs from the north face like steps. The top seems like a table, and from there it falls like a wall to the desert floor, a steep drop." He pauses a moment for the picture to take shape between us, like a mirage coming clear. "Impregnable! But so was Jotapata and many other fortresses. Even Jerusalem!" he gloats. "So, how shall we attack?" He does not want my answer, full of words himself. "The battering ram, of course. With this multitude of expendable prisoners, we could easily build a ramp."

He laughs, pleased by the irony of his next thought. "It always amuses me, Flavius, using the Jews against each other. They carry the water and supplies for us. They will build for us, and for what? To help us kill their brothers. And why? So they may live one more pitiful day!"

The scorn in his voice and the chuckle of satisfaction that comes from him as he turns these ideas over in his head anger me, for though it is my purpose to take this fortress, as it has been to subdue revolt elsewhere in Judea, I do not like to kill unnecessarily.

"Perhaps these Jews will choose to surrender," I offer, playing into his hands deliberately, for I know how he must respond.

He looks at me first with surprise, then with anger. "We must not allow them such a choice. They have used Masada as a base for raids against our troops; they have attacked towns where the inhabitants have sworn allegiance to Rome! Those loyal dead must be avenged!"

"You will remember, Marius," I say, dismissing him

13

curtly with my tone, "who is commander here, and who is under command. Regardless of what you feel or think, it is *I* who gives the orders!" He studies me with undisguised contempt, but his eyes veil quickly like a snake's, and with a sharp salute he turns and gallops back to his men.

Understand, I am not soft. But there has been enough killing, enough bloodshed. I do not admire the Jews; their stubborn belief in one god, when there are many, as everyone knows, revolts me. Yet, when Masada falls, all of Judea will come under my rule. It will be a time to return to sanity.

That these Zealots who live on Masada are desperate, I can well understand. But it is said that they are a people who believe in the sacredness of life, who love freedom with a fire, and who have fought for that freedom for six years, since the war began. Might they not listen to reason and surrender? The rest of their nation has been defeated. None remain to come to their defense. Now they are alone.

If we must fight to bring them to submission, fight we will. But by struggling, what have the Jews to gain? The battle is already won. Surely, then, they will surrender.

Chapter III

Surrender, or fight? I remember these thoughts filled my mind as I listened to the tramp of a Roman legion, watched the desert dust rise beneath their feet, dust like a breath of death.

What would be the will of our people, I wondered as we finally reached the top terrace and made our way around the wall separating the palace from the rest of Masada.

I have heard my father, Eleazar, and Rabbi Hillel argue long into the night about the right course of action, often falling asleep to the rise and fall of their voices in abstract debate. The debate would not be abstract now, I knew, as we hurried past the bath house and storage rooms, joining a stream of others who rushed to the place where everyone seemed to be moving.

In no time, that place became a restless sea of people, each in his own way responding to the crisis. John, Aram, and I joined a group of men who had been trained in the use of arms by my father. We stood together silently, awaiting his orders. Sara and Deborah sought out their mothers and also waited, wide-eyed and anxious, with the women along the walls. An old man wailed, "We are doomed, for we have transgressed!" Children cried in terror, sensing the unvoiced anxiety in other faces, alert to the difference in touch from their mothers, for some clutched their children fiercely, as though even at this moment the Romans were at our walls. An old woman sobbed as if for us all, "Jerusalem, Jerusalem!"

Despite these cries, the plateau seemed eerily quiet. I cannot account for it — unless it was that we all listened. I know myself that my ears strained to hear what my eyes could not see. My every sense was concentrated on that distant, persistent thud. And so it seemed with most in the crowd. All other sound seemed an intrusion on the relentless pounding of soldiers' feet.

Still, the old man's prophecy of doom — repeated again and again — was beginning to have its effect on the shocked and silent women, and I wanted to clap my hand to his mouth. No need. My father's voice rang out.

"Silence, old man!" he commanded coldly. "We will hear no more of this talk of doom. There is much work to be done."

My father, Eleazar ben Ya'ir, is a tall man with a face that is old for his years. His hair is thin and graying, and a muscle twitches in his left check when he is stressed, as it did now. As he stood atop the casemate wall, above one of the rooms in which our people lived, his manner was assured, and I could feel the tension around me ease. Though I could not see his eyes from where I stood, I knew the look they held, for I had seen it many times in his discussions with Rabbi Hillel. His gray eyes, which could look over the Sabbath candles to my mother with such tenderness, would be narrow and uncompromising now; his face, with its twitching muscle, would be tense with determination, his lips drawn in a tight line.

The silence that met his words made the pounding of marching feet clearer, for the air here is strange. Sound carries from great distances. One can hear each note of a bird's song from the desert floor far below.

My father recognized the panic that stirred in us all, but he too turned his head in the direction of the sound. Then, when he had heard enough, his voice drew us back to him.

"There will be no more tears." He spoke with calm. "There will be no more denial, either, for the Romans have come.

"Yes, the Romans have come! Did you think they would not? Did the years of peace in this place convince you that you were safe? Listen well. The sounds you hear now are as whispers to the noise they will make in months to come. Listen well; then dismiss these sounds, for if you let them dwell in your minds, you will become but whimpering cowards, not the iron-willed men of courage needed now. We are the last of our people. We must gird ourselves for the fight ahead. For fight we must, that those before us should not have died without purpose."

As my father paused for the solemnity of his words to find their mark, I recognized a stirring in the nearby crowd. Then, from its midst came Rabbi Hillel's voice, deep and soothing, caressing the crowd like a blessing.

"There must be no more bloodshed, Eleazar," he said, speaking directly to my father. "Many thousands of our people have died already. Do we have arms to fight these Roman soldiers? Do we have supplies to hold out against a long siege, should it come? Have we such cunning that we can achieve what our brothers could not against such odds? I say there has been enough bloodshed! If it were

17

God's will that his people should defeat the Romans, surely Jerusalem would not have fallen! How can we expect God to favor us now? Have we not broken his commandments? Have we not killed? Stolen? Broken the Sabbath?" He paused a moment in contemplation, then with a quiet certainty that came of deep conviction, he spoke for all to hear. "We must surrender!"

"No!" A voice screamed in me, echoing my father's words. Until that moment, I had not known my own heart. I looked to Aram and John, and each of them reflected my shock at Rabbi Hillel's command.

"No!" my father repeated.

"Yes, Eleazar," the rabbi said, his rich voice husky with emotion. "If for no other reason than survival. If we are all killed, who will carry on our faith? For thirty-five hundred years the Jews have lived and died in this land. It is most important that we live. The war is over. We have lost. What purpose would we serve by prolonging the outcome another few months? If we yield now, many lives will be saved. Some mercy may be shown. Some of us may live. Any life is preferable to death." He spoke passionately yet reasonably, and many heads turned in his direction.

"No!" my father repeated firmly. "Nothing has changed. Six years ago we opposed the Romans because they wronged us, because they withdrew our freedoms little by little, because they gradually forced their will upon us. 'Hear, O Israel, the Lord is One!' That is our central belief! One God. Yet the Romans dragged our wise men to their knees before their gods! Man can stand so much of such indignities, and if he does not rebel, he is no more a man. No! The reasons for our rebellion are as true now as ever. Nothing has changed!"

"You are wrong, Eleazar," the rabbi returned. "Everything has changed. Thousands of our people have died. But those who live can hope. No matter how terrible their lives, they draw sweet breath, and even if they must submit now, a day will come when they can be Jews again. *There is no hope in death.*"

"You think the Romans offer life?" My father laughed bitterly. "Do you not hear the marching? A legion of soldiers — and with them, ten thousand Jewish prisoners! Is that living? Those prisoners — our people — haul the lumber that will become platforms for the missile throwers. They are the beasts of burden for the enemy who will first destroy us, and then turn on them. What do you imagine is their fate? Life? Freedom? They too will die — but in the arenas, fighting wild animals, or worse, fighting each other, brother against brother, killing to live another day. Is that a better way to die than fighting here to the death? And their women — their wives and daughters. What is their fate? If they are strong, they will work until they drop, torn from their children who will be sold into slavery. If they are young, they will be bartered in markets as concubines for rich Syrians. Is this a choice?"

Like swords, my father's words hung over the crowd, unanswered, for there was no answer to what each knew to be true. The sound of marching feet grew louder. The people stood hypnotized by the heat, the approaching menace, the terrible, impossible choice.

"We must decide. Once and for all," my father said. "We cannot be divided now by indecision. Who says surrender? A show of hands!"

Only a few hands went up. He waited longer, knowing such a decision is not easily reached.

"Eleazar, wait!" Rabbi Hillel's voice again rang out. "Before you ask this, be sure your choice is clear. Let it be known beyond doubt that your road leads only one way — to death!" The stillness that followed was so great that I felt as if I stood on this rock fortress alone. After a long while, my father said, "A show of hands from those who say we fight!"

I raised my hand high so it might be counted clearly, and as far as I could see, all held their hands high, until the sea of people looked like spears struck in the ground. There was no need to count, and as my father's eyes swept over us, he announced, "Then we will fight! And such a fight we will make, the Romans will not soon forget. Let those who come after say of us we lived as men, and if we must die, then let it be said we fought well and died not slaves, but free."

Chapter IV

My father's confidence was contagious. Almost before he had finished speaking, a spirit of comradeship and hope pervaded the crowd. Even I felt a difference. All the tightness of a few moments before was gone, and in its place was strength. My body felt tireless, eager to be doing what must be done; my mind did not question the future. It knew! We would win. I was sure of it. I would question no longer. My heart said Eleazar was right, but when I thought ahead, my courage faltered. Action was the only answer now. In doing, there would be no time for thought. And once done, no going back.

Before this spirit of hope could wither, Eleazar issued orders. Even he seemed caught up in the excitement. The twitch in his face was gone. A small smile pulled at his lips. His eyes sparkled with the reflections of his fast-moving mind. His voice gained strength and warmth as thoughts and orders tumbled forth.

"We must make sure our water supply is adequate. After the Romans come, it will be increasingly difficult to bring the water up without being observed and fired upon. Berenice?" Eleazar called. My mother raised her hand in the crowd. "You will take as many women and children as you need to the cisterns and bring back enough water to replenish our storage tanks here."

"Aram," he directed, looking toward the group in which I stood. "You will go to the storage rooms and bring all remaining weapons to me at the headquarters building." Aram looked pleased. Though never tried in battle, he was our weapons expert, not only by necessity but by inclination. He had always shown a natural curiosity about weapons, their design and performance. Even when we were children, he listened for hours to the stories of passing tradespeople who told of the latest developments in Roman quick-loaders, or of the amazing accuracy of Cretan archers. That my father put him in charge of weapons now acknowledged this talent.

"John," my father next ordered. "Organize all fighting men into units of ten and meet me as soon as possible." John frowned, but his fair skin colored suddenly, and though his thick, dark brows nearly joined, I realized they masked his true reaction. John wasn't at all displeased. Though he shifted his tall frame from foot to foot in what might appear to be awkward embarrassment, he was already signaling, with a nod of the head or a raised finger, who was to join him when Eleazar finished.

"Check the lookout towers, Simon. See that each man knows his watch and where to report any unusual movement below. Then, back to me!"

I tried to swallow my disappointment. Was I, a man of seventeen, to be a messenger boy? Was this all the responsibility I would be given? I listened hard for more orders, but one by one the important tasks of leadership were given to others, and soon I found I could not look my father in the face.

22

And so it went. Women were called upon to tend our small fields, to organize stores of food, to prepare strips of linen as bandages, to keep the small children busy while the preparations for defense occupied their brothers and fathers. Many of the older people would spend their time in prayer, for no matter how well prepared we might be, the final outcome of our actions would be the will of God.

"And now," my father said, smiling at our people, "one thing further. Despite these preparations, some things will not change. We will continue to observe the Sabbath, and the holidays as well — within reason. Rabbi Hillel will see to that. The children will continue to attend school, because without knowledge, man is no better than an animal." The children groaned in disappointment, and their elders laughed. "As always, the sick, the poor, and the elderly will be properly cared for. And we will help each other in whatever ways we can."

Already a group was forming around my mother. Women disappeared into the apartments of the casemate wall and soon reappeared with large jugs. They were joined by children who were old enough to carry water but too young to bear arms.

Elsewhere, John stood counting men into groups of ten while his eyes searched the crowd for yet more of our fighting force. Suddenly, his look fixed on one form cutting its way through the clusters of people. It was Deborah, moving toward him with an urgency that drew my attention. When John caught sight of her, it was as though none else existed. His military manner vanished. He whispered orders briefly to a near lieutenant, then with like singleness of purpose ran to her. Once met, they stood unheeding while others brushed by, unaware even that I stood near. They spoke for but a moment. I could not hear their words, but John's gentle touch of Deborah's face said all. I could not watch any longer, feeling I intruded in too personal a matter. John has been as a brother, and Deborah a sister, to me, and though I had seen this growing care each had for the other, this crisis made their feelings clear. I was glad for them, glad they had found each other now, while there was still time. But in my heart I felt a void. I knew not why.

As the crowd dispersed, each to take up his assigned task, I turned toward the casemate wall that surrounds our fortress. It had a reassuring look, solid and gleaming white in the sunshine. The double walls are massive, each much thicker than the length of a man's arm. And they are tall, more than three times the height of a man. Between them are about a hundred rooms, but even so there is not space enough for all our people.

From the outside, the wall appears as an unbroken line, almost one with the mountain on which it rises. Yet there are ways to leave Masada, as I have said before. With John I have often gone through the snake-path gate and down the winding way to the valley below, and thence to near and distant Roman settlements. Our fighting zeal is well appreciated by those who have known our visits, I think. But there can be no more such forays now.

In more peaceful times, we have journeyed with other young people to Ein Gedi, leaving by the west gate sometimes. The waterfalls and the spring there provided refreshment in the hot time of the year, and the palm fronds we brought back were woven into many bearing baskets by our women. These trips too can be no more.

The casemate wall has two more exits, which were crowded now with people rushing through to reach the cisterns in the sides of our hill before darkness came. The paths from the water gates are difficult and narrow, but the twelve huge caverns carved in the rock by Herod's engineers hold so much water that the trip is well worth the effort.

Above the casemate wall rise thirty-eight towers at intervals along its length, and each reaches three or four times higher than the wall itself. It was to one of these I hurried now, climbing the outside stairs leading to the ramparts, and then into the first tower. Through its window could be seen a slice of land and the Sea of Salt, now misted in late afternoon heat, shrouding the mountains on the opposite side from Masada. I made my way from tower to tower, checking with each sentry, alerting him to his job, assuring him with a certainty I did not feel that we would stand against the Romans as no others had yet done.

The young believed my words, too innocent to question the authority of Eleazar's son. It was the older men who watched my face with unrevealing eyes, knowing better than I what was in store for us.

The difference in attitude between young and old always interests me. If I could not see a man, but knew his thought, I could roughly tell his age. On guard in one of the towers was a young man, perhaps fifteen years old, Aram's age. Like desert grass, his beard was just beginning to show, and he stroked the sparse growth incessantly, as though he could hasten nature into making him a man.

"Simon," he asked anxiously as soon as I entered his tower room, "what is it like to fight? Are you afraid? What if you cannot kill when the enemy is upon you? What if your hand will not raise the sword? How can I fight when God has said, 'Thou shall not kill'!"

He turned from me and looked intently through the narrow window of the tower for a moment, then continued. "Have you ever thought . . ." — and his eyes would not meet mine — "Have you ever thought that you might *like* to kill?" I think his own words surprised him, for he shook his head as if in disbelief. His forehead puckered, and his hand stayed fixed on the young chin.

"I mean . . . I love my brother. Yet there have been times when I have hated him so fiercely that I believe I could have . . . killed him. I truly hate the Romans. What if this violence within me is my real nature? What if I find . . ." — and he searched for the right words, almost whispering them in shame at his thoughts — "that I *can* kill after all, that . . . I find it satisfying?"

I put my hand on his shoulder, feeling very old. "We all wonder these things," I said, "thinking ourselves cowardly, or courageous, but not really knowing what we are until the moment when action decides for us."

I remembered the doubts I had suffered — only three years ago? — in Jerusalem. The Romans had broken into the lower city, and to protect the women and children while they sought higher ground, we stayed and fought. I was younger than this boy here, and just as frightened and untried. I did not think I could kill another, even an enemy. Until the moment when I turned into a street where a Roman soldier was dragging an old, wounded man by his bloodied beard, handling him like a sack of sand that stands in the way. Seeing this careless brutality, this outrageous indignity, drove me to fury. I drew my sword and, with a savagery I never dreamed possible, ran it through the soldier's body. And still not content, I drew out the sword and thrust again and again, all the time crying with hatred and revulsion. I killed many times that day, and each kill came easier than the last. My hands performed acts entirely foreign to my nature, but only because my mind was numb. I never enjoyed killing.

The doubt and eagerness of the young sentry stood in sharp contrast to the response of the old man I met later in one of the towers to the south. His eyes were keen, or he would not have been assigned as a lookout. Even so, he was occupying one of the least sensitive posts, for it was unlikely that any danger would arise from the south: the terrain is too rough, the rock too steep.

When I entered his tower, he was seated on a stone bench near the window, reading his prayers. He seemed not at all disturbed that I had found him thus disposed. In fact, if anything, he acted as though my coming were an intrusion. He listened quietly while I reminded him of his duty and told him briefly of the discussion between my father and Rabbi Hillel. There was no fear, no doubt at all in his manner. "I am an old man and have lived a good life," he said to me as I left. "For me it does not matter anymore. But God go with *you*, my son." His resignation was more distressing to me than all the young man's doubts.

I stopped last at the northernmost towers, where the sentries watched with special interest as the Roman army below halted for the night, only a short day's walk away. As I gazed down into the darkening desert, I could not help but wonder at the efficiency of these Roman legions, even in this routine matter of setting up camp. In no time at all, sites were marked and tents erected, the horses corraled and set to feed. I could not see with clarity the layout of their camp, for the light fails fast. Still, the wide dispersion of their cooking fires seemed to cover miles of what only yesterday was desolate, rock-strewn land best known to vipers, jackals, and an occasional lion.

Chapter V

I met my younger brother as I left the last tower and returned to the plateau. He was distributing weapons from one of the many storage rooms to men who were carrying away as many as they could hold. "I'll be finished here soon," Aram called out above the babble of voices and the clank of weaponry. "Can you wait? I need to talk with you."

I joined him in the storage room, where he stood surrounded by hundreds of shields, knives, bows, and arrows. He grasped a spear and ran a hand knowingly along its shaft. "Herod may have been a tyrant king," he said, "but he was also a very frightened one. He left enough weapons here to supply a whole legion, maybe two."

"A whole legion! Six thousand men! And what have we? Six hundred?"

"Oh no — hardly that!" he quickly answered. "Four hundred at best."

We looked at each other, figuring the odds. Maybe twelve to one if you counted only the Roman legionaries.

Thirty-six to one if you counted the mercenaries and the Jewish prisoners. "Well," Aram said, "David slew Goliath with worse odds than that. Besides, we have superior position." He strode past me and signaled the guard to lock the door. "That counts for something."

"We have another thing in our favor," I said, only half-joking. "No place else to run."

"Which counts for something, too, I suppose," Aram said distractedly. "But that is not what I need to speak about."

We hurried along the street that passed the storage rooms. There was still considerable traffic in supplies. People scurried like mice at the approach of winter, in and out of the various rooms collecting grain, dried fruits, wine, and other foodstuffs in anticipation of shortages. The memory of the famine in Jerusalem was all too vivid yet. Now that we would be unable to leave the fortress, some sort of food rationing would have to be put into effect quickly.

As we neared the building that serves as both administration headquarters and living quarters for our family, Aram stopped and grasped my arm. "I want you to be the first to know, Simon," he said. "I am going to ask father if Sara and I may be betrothed and married soon." His face shone even in the near darkness. "Do you think it is the wrong time? I mean, now that the Romans have come, it seems like there are more important things to be thinking about, and doing . . . But . . ." He let his words die away, finding it hard to think of anything more important to him than marrying Sara.

Aram had been promised to another, a marriage arranged by our parents when he was yet a child. In ordinary times, he would have met his bride for the first time just before the wedding ceremony. "Love comes after marriage, not before" is the belief of our people. But his future wife died in Jerusalem before we left.

Here at Masada, our living conditions are different from those of the cities where we lived before. We mingle more in this crowded place, and we find it difficult to hold to every custom as before. Though many of the old disapprove of what they call our moral decay, I believe this new freedom of communication between young men and women to be a good thing. It was only natural, because of it, that Aram and Sara grew to know each other as friends and were already in love. My father would likely approve the betrothal and marriage, because Sara comes from a scholarly family, and so the match is a good one.

Looking into the anxious face of my brother, I wanted to reassure him about the timing of his decision. I embraced him happily and offered my congratulations. "There could be no better time, Aram," I said earnestly, realizing that this was really true. "A wedding is just what we need now! It will take people's minds off their fears."

The large inner courtyard of the apartment building in which we lived was crowded with men. (These quarters had served as barracks for Roman officers when their troops had been garrisoned here some years ago. One of our soldiers, probably on my father's orders, sat at a small table near the entrance to our apartment. He was listening to the appeal of each of the men who wished to see my father, deciding who would gain audience with him. At a nearby apartment, a group of elders gathered in serious discussion around the rabbi. They no doubt would be considering what to do with the sacred scrolls in the event of our possible defeat. They would also discuss whether or not to gather the yearly tithe, which each adult Jew must contribute to the maintenance of the Temple. Our

Temple in Jerusalem has fallen, but the half shekel each of us contributes will someday build another.

We were admitted to my father's room at once, for he had been asking for us already. The door was closed against the outside noise, and the heat became oppressive. This room normally served as our sitting and dining place. Adjoining were two small sleeping rooms. My mother worked in a corner, preparing pomegranate juice. She looked weary from the long afternoon of carrying water from the cisterns. When she brought the pitcher to my father, I saw that her hands were stained almost the color of blood. My father said, "Go, Berenice, and rest. You look very weary. We will be a while yet, and will see to food ourselves." My mother smoothed her hair, which she wore in a knot behind her head, and touched my father lightly. When she turned to leave the room, her shoulders sagged. But even her weariness could not hide the fact that she is a handsome woman, tall and graceful, with an elegant bearing. And though educated only in the things women are expected to know, she has taught herself to read and write.

My father had been waiting for us before hearing the reports. Now he turned to the men around him and asked what each had learned.

"There is enough food at Masada to last one year, perhaps longer, if we are careful," one man said.

"What about water?" my father asked.

"The upper cisterns are full. There should be no need to replenish them for perhaps a month. Then it can be done at night. Still, we do not know if this will be a wet year, so we should consider allotting both food and water cautiously."

"Simon." My father turned to me. "Work out a fair

system of rationing." Another small task, I thought, stiffening. "Aram? How about the weapons?"

"We have enough for everyone," Aram said immediately. "The real question is whether we will be able to use them. From what I know of Roman methods, it will take ingenuity to do them much damage, and a miracle to gain the upper hand."

"But we have the better physical position," another man remarked. "In a month — two at most — we will have them on the rout."

"Hah!" Aram laughed mirthlessly. "You have much to learn!"

"We may be able to hold them," my father said hopefully, warning Aram to silence with his look. "With God's help, we will." He turned to John. "How do we stand in manpower?"

"About four hundred men," John answered immediately, "of which half are prime soldiers, trained by you, sir. The rest are either over age, or infirm, or really too young, but in an emergency all can be counted on in some way."

"Very good," Eleazar said, hurrying on. "About tomorrow. We can expect the enemy to reach the base of Masada by sundown. It will be some time before they are able to do any damage, which puts us in the stronger position. Now, John has offered a suggestion." He looked to my friend with approval. "I will let him tell you about it."

John reddened slightly. Unaccustomed to being the center of attention, he had never been one at ease with words. He glanced my way as though looking for encouragement, which was ever there. But truly, the approval in my father's voice had given him that.

"We have made our decision to fight," John said, "so

there is no reason why we should not show these invaders that the Jews of Masada are not afraid. More — that we will not be defeated! When they have assembled at the base of the rock, as they will — for that is how they attacked the fortresses in the Galilee — we will allow them to gather close. Then, as they raise their swords and let out that barbaric scream of theirs, we will send them our answer — in rocks!" He beamed, knowing by the looks on our faces what we thought of his idea.

I felt a surge of envy, but admiration too. It *was* a good plan! Bold, imaginative, just the sort of opening move that would give us immediate advantage.

Eleazar spoke now. "As John has pointed out to me, this action will achieve two things: It will show the Romans we feel confident of our strength, which will demoralize them; and it will give our people their first taste of success, while committing them once and for all to fight to the finish!"

John took our praise with good-natured humor. We gathered round him as if he were a hero, slapped him on the back, and called him "general." He laughed at our extravagant words and modestly insisted we each would have thought of it had we thrown as many pebbles over the ramparts as he had.

Commander John! I was proud of my friend and glad to see how well he took to leadership. Only this morning his sole concern had been for his farm in the Galilee. Not our people. Not freedom. Not survival. How much he had changed in one day!

Our jubilant mood was suddenly interrupted. We turned away from John to see that a young boy now stood by my father's table. The boy had entered the room while we were congratulating John and seemed anxious to be gone.

"This boy brings a message from Ananus ben Ezra," my father said. "He is urgently in need of help. It seems many of our people have suddenly taken ill, and ben Ezra has not enough hands to cope. Who will go to help?" He looked around at each of the men in the room. His eyes settled on me. "You have always been caring with people," he said. "Will you go, Simon?"

My heart raced with excitement. Surely my face showed how I felt. To work with Ananus ben Ezra, one of the finest physicians from Jerusalem, would be a privilege, not a duty.

"Of course," I said, before another might apply. "I will go."

Chapter VI

Ananus ben Ezra lived near the snake-path gate in one of the casemate rooms. He could have enjoyed better housing in a more spacious building on Masada, and certainly more privacy, but he chose to be near those who needed him.

A line of people curved along the wall that led to his chamber. In the darkness, lit by those holding oil lamps, one could see huddled shapes and hear sounds of terrible distress. Some held their hands to their bellies and groaned. Others, listless and pale, sat on the ground.

The physician's young daughter strode up and down the line of people, reassuring them that they would soon be helped. His wife interviewed those nearest the entrance, asking about their complaints and relaying this information to her husband.

Ananus ben Ezra was a short, thin man with a head of wild gray hair falling into a beard a little like that of a goat. I found him seated on a stool facing a patient in his chamber. Several oil lamps lit the room. The patient's daughter stood nearby. He nodded to me to take a seat.

". . . and when did this sickness first begin, old mother?" he asked kindly, holding the patient's thin, wrinkled hand.

Though the night was warm, the woman shivered uncontrollably. "Soon after Eleazar's talk to us."

"She cannot keep food down," her daughter interjected. "Nothing. Not even water."

The physician nodded. He held his palm to the old woman's forehead, put his ear to her chest. Then he listened to her rapid, wheezing breaths. Suddenly the woman began to heave, her whole frail body shuddering with the effort, and the doctor hastily proffered a basin. His face displayed deep concern as he supported the old woman, who strained forward, gasping and retching. At last her vomiting ceased; her shaking subsided. She sat bent, limp, exhausted.

"Do you feel better now?" he asked, as the daughter removed the basin. She barely nodded, and tears pooled in her eyes.

"We should not have come," her daughter said. "It is the plague. There is no helping her."

Ananus ben Ezra's face assumed a look of stern disapproval. Again he took the old woman's hand in his and, addressing the daughter, scolded, "You must not think such thoughts! Have you ever seen plague?"

"When I was a small child," she replied, her back to the doctor.

"Then how do you account for the fact that your mother has no fever? See for yourself. She is cool."

"If it is not the plague, then it is poison," she insisted stubbornly.

"Why would anyone wish to poison your good mother? She is loved by all who know her."

"It is the Romans," she explained impatiently, gestur-

36

ing vaguely toward the door. "Do you not see how many of our people are ill? They have poisoned our water!"

I dared to interrupt. "But how is that possible? They have not yet arrived."

She regarded me shrewdly. My reasoning made no impression. Her voice grew surer. "Today we drew water from the cisterns. Tonight everyone who drinks water is sick. They must have sent spies ahead of their legion to poison us while we slept, before we knew of their coming."

"This kind of reasoning is dangerous," the doctor protested, "and it is false! Surely you noticed too that no children are ill. Did they not drink the water also?"

The young woman opened her mouth to speak, then closed it and frowned.

Ananus ben Ezra turned to the old mother again. He stroked her hand gently and studied her face. She sighed. "Are you afraid, mother?" he asked softly. "Afraid of the Romans?" Her dull gray eyes glanced quickly toward her daughter; then, almost imperceptibly, she nodded.

The daughter, unaware of her mother's admission, said, "If it is not poison, then it is a Roman curse."

"Let it be a curse, then," the doctor said, resigned. "Now you must go home and pray that this curse will be lifted. And it *will* be, as soon as we strike the first blow. You will see. And good mother — do not drink or eat anything until morning. Then you will be well again."

When they had left, and before the next patient was admitted, the doctor welcomed me and explained, "Tonight I have seen three types of illness. The stomach disorder, as you yourself just witnessed, the heart and rapid pulse complaints, and the skin eruptions that cover most of the patient's body with welts the size of shekels."

"They are all due to fear?" I asked.

"I think so, though I cannot be certain. Of course, each patient has his own explanation: the plague, heart failure, the pox, poison — everything except the real culprit. The Romans."

"Could a curse have caused the illness?"

"No. And it is hard to admit to fear." The doctor smiled quietly to himself. "A curse can be lifted. Would that the Romans could be disposed of so easily." He shook his head. "By morning we will all be ready to accept the Romans' presence. As soon as we can do something about it, I think there will be no more of this kind of sickness."

I spent the rest of the evening assisting Ananus ben Ezra. I sat in an adjoining room, listening as patient after patient complained of the same symptoms the doctor had described. We could do little except reassure these people that they would be better in the morning and that they were not victims of the plague.

When the last patient had gone, Ananus ben Ezra offered me a slice of nut cake and a cup of goat's milk. It was late. His wife and daughter had gone to bed.

He dipped the cake into the milk and regarded me closely. "You did well with the patients, Simon," he said. "Understanding, but firm. You would make a good teacher." He drank a mouthful of foaming milk. "Or physician," he added, smiling at me over the lip of his cup.

"I have always wished to be a doctor," I said, too interested in this conversation to care about the refreshments. "But I never considered it possible. The future has been so uncertain, our lives so disrupted by the war."

"True," he said thoughtfully. "At your age I was well into my studies at the medical school in Alexandria. That is not an opportunity open to you now. But why not" — and he looked at me curiously — "yes, why could you not apprentice to me, if you truly wish to study medicine? You could be of great help, for I have much more of a load than I can carry at my age. Can Eleazar spare you?"

I thought of the routine task I had been assigned, checking the sentries at the towers. It was a job that, once done, took little time. I thought too of the assignment I now had to organize the rationing of food and water. But once organized, that would run itself.

I would ask my father what his plans were for me. Perhaps I was needed as a soldier. But if only I could work with the doctor!

I left Ananus ben Ezra's quarters with a sense of unreality. Forgotten was the immediate menace of the Romans. I wanted to hold fast this feeling of elation, of having a usefulness and purpose that I had never known before.

The evening was still warm, though a slight cooling breeze blew from the south. The sky was brilliant with stars, and the moon so bright that I could have read by it, had I a scroll before me. It was late, much later than our usual time for sleep, but most people were too anxious to rest now. Many had set up stools outside their warm sleeping rooms. Many were still strolling about as though they were in a large city in the midst of a summer evening.

I felt so restless, so alive, too alert to rest. Too full of a sense of immortality to allow sleep to break the spell. A doctor! It was such a rare feeling, this sense of hope, of having a future, that I felt reluctant to seek out a friend and put it into words, afraid that its magic might dissipate. Instead of returning to my room, I made my way to Herod's palace, racing quickly down the hundreds of stairs to the lowest terrace, where John, Deborah, and I had spoken only this morning.

There, against the outer wall, I stood, face up to the starlit sky, smiling at my good fortune, tasting the awe I felt at the word "physician." I thought I was alone, but suddenly I became aware of another standing nearby.

"Simon?" Deborah's voice called softly. "Is that you?"

She came to where I stood, and together we looked out upon the starry night.

We stood quietly thus for a long moment. Then she said, as though to herself, "Did Herod stand here a hundred years ago, as we do now? Who will look out upon this view a hundred years from now . . . a thousand, or perhaps two? We are such insignificant specks in terms of time." She shook her head. "After we are gone, these stars will still shine. This rock will still stand."

She was silent again for a time, then added pensively, "Yet we think everything that happens to us here is so terribly important!"

"And is it not?" I asked, ready now to speak about my recent experience. "Tonight I learned that it is possible for me to become a doctor. And I will become one. I will! Despite the Romans. Despite the war! Whether or not my father approves. I will!"

My determination must have been ferocious, for she chuckled. I turned to her, annoyed that she could find humor in my seriousness.

"Why do you laugh?" I asked sternly. "There is nothing laughable about my words!"

"It is you, Simon. I have never seen you so sure of yourself." Her eyes sparkled with mischief. "You are always the one who bends with the wind, who does whatever no one else will do, just to prevent argument. Suddenly you know so surely what you want and where you are going. You were so . . ." and her hand swayed back and forth as she searched for the right words.

"Now," she said, and her voice grew deep and exaggerated in its seriousness, "you are a lion!" Again she laughed.

True. Until this moment, I had lived as directed. If there was need for a farmer, I was a farmer. If there was need for a teacher, or a soldier, or a messenger, or anything else, I would be that for a time, doing as well as I could but with no special heart for it. But in a day all that had changed. No one could make me be anything else now that I saw what was possible.

"Do not be angry, Simon," she said gently. "I am glad that you have found your direction. So much has happened today. Even I have found something important to me. Someone. John."

She turned to look toward the stairs behind us, thinking she had heard a step. "He was to meet me here, but perhaps he is too busy, arranging for tomorrow. It is too late now, anyway. I do not think he will come." She sighed.

I watched her face as it became absorbed in the lights of the Roman campfires below. She had a high forehead, and her dark, straight hair swept back from it in a smooth line. Her olive skin always had rich color; her intelligent eyes were slanted slightly, like those of Orientals. It was a different face, one I never tired of seeing, for it reflected the many backgrounds of our people.

As she became aware of my intense gaze, she turned her head, and the light caught the gloss of her lips. My heart suddenly beat more quickly, and I caught my breath at the sight of her loveliness, and the nearness of her, and the strangeness of being alone together at this hour, which our law forbids.

Her arm brushed mine as she turned, and I moved away brusquely, feeling an anguish I cannot describe. My arms ached to hold her, to bring her sweetness close to me. Reason argued, "Do not touch. It is forbidden. And she is John's." But another kind of fire burned within me, destroying reason.

"What is it, Simon?" Deborah asked anxiously. "You look so strange. So . . . fierce. Are you still angry?"

I shook my head, not daring speak for fear my voice would betray me. She studied me a while, then turned back to watch the dying campfires below, and spoke low, as though we were the last two people in the world.

"You have known John a long time, Simon. What is your opinion of him?"

What does one say at such a time? What one really thinks, or what he knows the other wishes to hear? I knew John well, and he was my friend, but what I knew as good qualities before now seemed serious flaws. In his loyalty and dependability, I saw stolidity. His slowness to anger seemed less a virtue than a lack of imagination; his gentleness, an absence of fire. His willingness to listen without comment suggested he had no words of his own.

And Deborah was quite the opposite. She missed no tone of voice or subtlety of word. Her speech was rich, her observations keen, her curiosity boundless. She had a wildness in her too, an untamed, seeking quality unusual in our women. Where others walked with eyes downcast, submissive, obedient, unquestioning, she strode with her head high, as impulsive and open as a child.

Was she too "fine" for John? And was that for me to say?

"He is my friend," I said at last. "John is a good man. As solid as the earth. He could make you happy."

"Yes, that is what I think too," Deborah said, pleased. "Do you know how many times my family has moved in my fifteen years? Seven! Seven times! From Rome to Alexandria to Scythopolis to Caesarea, Tiberias, Jerusalem, and now to Masada. I feel like a — nomad! No sooner do I weave the threads of life in one place than we must unravel those threads and move on to another.

"Do you know that John has lived *all* of his life in one place in the Galilee — until he came here, I mean. And his family, too, back three hundred years or more. Imagine! He is almost a part of the land." She shook her head in wonder.

"There is something so solid and sure about that. He is no nomad. He is a rock! A tree with deep roots. There is a sense of continuity in him. He will farm his lands, as his father did, and as our children will do. There is something beautiful in that."

"Is that why you love John?" I asked, amazed to realize Deborah knew nothing of love, that all her reasons were wrong.

She thought again a moment, then said, "I am tired of uncertainty, and he is hope. He makes me feel there will always be a tomorrow. Yes, that is why."

My heart began to race again. My lips were dry. "But that is no reason to love someone, Deborah!" I exclaimed, frightened at what I had dared to say.

"You think not? Have you a better reason, Simon?" she challenged.

I searched her face and could hardly abide her look of fierce determination. But gradually, as our gaze held, some inner doubt long dormant in her suddenly awoke, and tears welled in her eyes.

A better reason. Yes, I thought. And heedless of propriety, conscience, reason, and loyalty, I stepped forward now and took her in my arms.

Like a startled dove, she struggled to escape. I brought her close, captured in my embrace, and waited as her first distress became acceptance, surprise, and then wonder. When I kissed her lips, her body, suddenly attentive, sensed mine, and responded to it. Soon my mind no longer listened or functioned. And all I could do was murmur, "Deborah. Deborah. I love you."

Chapter VII

The Romans' progress toward Masada was reported regularly the next day and observed by all who could crowd onto the northern ramparts and onto the terraces of the palace.

The doctor was right. Once our people took action, all signs of illness disappeared. As soon as they learned of John's plan to bombard the Romans with rocks, everyone tried to outdo his neighbor in searching out and bringing to the top of the casemate walls the largest, most destructive stones. Those who could not find any lying about dug for them. Even children hardly old enough to walk picked up small pebbles and offered them to their parents. A cache of rocks the size of large melons was hauled up from Herod's storerooms and readied for the assault. There seemed to be a holiday feeling in the atmosphere, yet also a growing and disturbing frenzy. People laughed too often and too hard. Tears came too readily from laughter.

Overnight, John had become a hero, a Zealot leader,

his name on everyone's lips. "He is one to be listened to, that young man," I heard men say with pride.

No one seemed ready to think beyond today. The immediate action held their complete attention. They seemed unaware that this was something committing us irrevocably to war.

I did not see Deborah in the morning, for I began my work with Ananus ben Ezra. He spent the time introducing me to the herbal and medicinal remedies he used most commonly, and instructed me in the use of the basic tools of his profession, tools I would not come to use for a long time.

My father readily gave consent to work with the doctor. After only brief consideration he had said, "It is good that you learn a profession. You have always had an inquiring mind and a caring way with people, so this seems right for you. But you must be available in special emergencies."

My brother Aram did not agree. Though glad for my opportunity, he was a realist.

"What good will it do, Simon?" he asked bitterly. "How long do you think we can hold out against the Romans? A month? Two?"

My father tried to silence him with a stern look, but Aram would not heed. "It is a waste of time," he said, "saving life, prolonging life, bringing life into this world, when soon we will all be dead!"

"Aram — enough!" my father warned, the tick in his cheek beginning again as he saw the look of pain in my mother's eyes. "If that were true, why bother to fight at all? If you give up believing there is a chance for us, why do you want to marry Sara?"

"To have something before I die!" he cried. "These last six years! Nothing but blood and terror — and loss!"

His voice broke. My mother moved to his side and placed a hand on his shoulder. He shook her off. There was a long silence in the room. At last, my mother sighed.

"I slept little last night. Maybe it is fatigue," Aram said, trying to make amends. Then, without conviction, and with downcast eyes, he added, "I am sorry, Simon. You will make a fine doctor."

There was truth in what Aram said about our future and in what my father said about hope. I believed both truths, but today, with the prospect of studying medicine before me, and the joy of last night's encounter with Deborah still like a fire within me, my father's argument seemed the wiser.

I longed to see Deborah later in the day, before the call went out for all to gather on the parapet. I glimpsed her earlier, as she led a group of children to the wheat field, where they would empty the heavy jugs of water they carried. It seemed strange she did not hear me call, for the children around her pulled at her dress and turned in my direction. But eyes straight ahead, she walked on, her step quickening.

It puzzled me, but I did not think much of it until later. Then I saw her with John. The way they spoke together, with John leaning one arm on the wall against which she stood, brought fear to my heart. Had she not told him how she felt now? Did last night's embrace mean nothing to her after all? Had I imagined she cared?

At last I found her, seated in the shade of a pomegranate tree, surrounded by children. The Romans had already begun to encircle the rock. She knew it. But the children did not. She pressed her fingers to her lips to silence me while she finished relating the story of Moses receiving the Ten Commandments. I watched her animated face with pleasure. The children leaned toward her, eyes fixed on her face. When she came at last to the end of the story, they released their breath in unison, and only then did their attention wander.

"But Deborah," a boy asked, "if God said, 'Thou shalt not kill,' and 'Thou shalt love thy neighbor as thyself,' why do we take rocks up to the wall? What are they for? Are not the Romans our neighbors? Do we not mean to kill them with those rocks?"

Deborah glanced at me, frowning. "Why do you think the Romans come here, Joshua?" she asked.

"My father said they want Masada," the child answered.

"You were too young to remember when the war began, Joshua. Or why it started. We have not spoken of that before, because I thought we were safe here. Maybe we should speak of it now."

"When did the war start, Deborah?" young voices asked.

"I will let Simon explain everything to you. Simon?" she said, indicating a seat on the ground near her with a graceful sweep of her hand.

How could we speak of these things now, with the enemy below, already encircling us? Deborah kept these children in a quiet little pocket, while the rest of Masada seethed with a strange mixture of terror and bravado. I could hear people running, voices raised in overexcited commands.

"Deborah!" I protested.

She knew my meaning instantly. "Simon, your father said that life must go on as near to normal as possible, even in the midst of war. Please tell the children why the war began."

I looked at these little ones, all six or younger, born since the war began, protected by their parents from the darkest knowledge. Yet children know more than adults imagine. How much should I say? Enough to help them understand why we must fight, but not enough to frighten them. I closed my eyes a moment to find the thread of thought I wished to follow.

"Have your fathers told you about the four kinds of men?" I began. Their young, fresh faces shone with curiosity. Many heads shook no.

"There is he who says, 'What is mine is mine, and what is thine is thine.' He is a good man. He who says 'What is mine is thine, and what is thine is mine' is a boor — a fool. He who says 'What is mine is thine, and what is thine is thine' is a saint. And he who says 'What is thine is mine, and what is mine is mine' is a wicked man. The Romans are wicked men. They gave us nothing but grief, and they took whatever they wished from us.

"Do you remember Florus?" I asked, unraveling another thread of thought. The Romans below ceased to exist. "No, you would not," I said. "Florus was the Roman procurator before you were born. A very wicked man. Do you know what he did? He encouraged robbers to steal from our people, and they shared what they stole with him. If our people caught the robbers, he sent his troops to punish *us*. He wanted us to revolt, for if we did, his troops could raid our cities and steal from our sacred treasury. But it was not only because of money that we fought back. It was because of injustice, and because, finally, there was no freedom at all for us."

Deborah sat with her hands cupping her face, eyes on me. Some children fidgeted, heads turned to the sound below, while others listened attentively.

"Tell them about Caesarea, Simon," Deborah encouraged.

I nodded. "The Jews of Caesarea wanted to buy the

49

land on which their synagogue was built, but the Greeks would not sell it to them. In fact, they built workshops all around the synagogue, until it was almost impossible to reach the entrance of the building. The Jews appealed to Florus, and he said, 'Give me eight talents of gold, and I will stop the Greeks from building more shops.' But Florus lied. He took the money and did nothing.

"One Sabbath, one of the Greeks set an earthen vessel, bottom up, at the entrance to the synagogue and began to sacrifice birds. Do you know what that means, children?" I went on. "It says in Leviticus that killing a bird in that way is to be done only to cleanse a leper. This Greek was telling the Jews they were all lepers.

"Some of our young people wanted to kill the Greek, but the elders said, 'No, let us first appeal to Florus. Then, if he does nothing, we should leave Caesarea and take with us our books of law.' When Florus heard these men's complaint, what do you think he did?"

"He punished the Greek?" one of the smaller children asked.

"Of course not, silly," the boy Joshua exclaimed with adult authority. "My father told me about that. He punished the Jewish elders for taking the books of law away to Jerusalem."

The other children's admiring looks made Joshua blush. "Very good, Joshua," Deborah said. "Can you tell us what happened next?"

The unexpected praise flustered the child. His plump, fair face reddened. His curly head dropped tight against his chest, where it remained. Immediately the others giggled at his embarrassment.

"Simon will continue," Deborah said, bringing a halt to their laughter. Fingers went into mouths, foreheads wrinkled in feigned deep thought, and eyes turned to study the ground in hopes of escaping Deborah's direct gaze.

The interruption brought me back to the present. It seemed mad to be telling stories to these children now, as the Romans drew their noose around us. "Deborah, this is not the time to talk of these things. I must see you alone for a moment," I said impatiently.

Her face flushed. "There is time, Simon," she whispered. "The call to go to the walls has not been sounded yet. Please tell them about Jerusalem now."

I began to speak again. It flashed through my mind that rather than argue, I was bending to the will of others again. It hurt to know I had not really changed.

"Florus left Caesarea and went to Jerusalem, demanding that those who spoke against him be delivered to him at once. Our elders begged, 'Forgive them. They are young and foolish.' But Florus did not listen. He ordered his men to plunder the upper marketplace and slay the people. Thirty-six hundred died that day. And he did one further thing that no one else had done before. He ordered Jewish men of the equestrian order put to death by being nailed to a cross.

"Even after such a terrible deed, our people struggled to keep the peace. The elders urged the rebellious to be patient, saying, 'Florus will not be procurator forever.' Soon after, Florus told the Jews to prove their loyalty by going out to greet Roman soldiers approaching the city. The high priests urged the people to do as Florus ordered rather than start a war.

"But what they didn't know was that Florus had sent a messenger ahead to the army, telling them to fight these Jews!"

Deborah interrupted hotly. "My father joined those who went out in peace to meet the soldiers and greet them. The soldiers listened to their words in silence. Then, without warning or reason, they turned on our people, clubbing them, trampling them with their horses, and pushing them back to the city."

I waited for Deborah to continue, but she sat quivering with rage and said no more.

"We accepted these terrible cruelties for almost three years," I continued, watching Deborah closely. "Finally we began to fight back. Some Jews, who lived outside of Judea, chose not to fight, for they had not lived and suffered under Florus as we had. And so, when we began to attack Roman strongholds, even to Scythopolis, Jews living there fought us as though *we* were their real enemies. These Jews killed many of our people, but did their loyalty matter to the citizens of Scythopolis? No! They asked the Jews to leave their city before more harm came to its inhabitants, and to prove their loyalty. After three nights in the woods outside the city, these thousands of loyal Jewish citizens of Scythopolis were attacked and killed by the Romans! Do you see why we must fight, now that the Romans have come here?"

Some of the children held their heads and cried for their mothers. It was a terrible thing to tell such little ones, but we could no longer protect them from the future. Better they should be armed with knowledge of why their fathers must fight.

Suddenly the sound of the shofar, the signal to assemble on the wall, blasted from the synagogue. It was repeated in all corners of the plateau.

"Go, children," Deborah said now, embracing each child quickly. "It is time to return to your mothers." She directed the children away.

She avoided my eyes and began to move away. "We had better go to the wall now, Simon," she said.

52

"Wait!" I commanded. "There will be two more warnings before they need us. Why do you rush away? Why have you been avoiding me? You have not told John about us, have you?"

She lowered her eyes. "What is there to say?"

I felt like shaking her. "Deborah! Did last night mean nothing to you?"

She raised her face, and tears shone in her eyes. "You had no right, Simon! It was wrong enough that we spoke together alone. You should not have touched me! And how could you wrong John so? You knew of his feelings for me. How could you do that to your friend, and to me?"

"If I offended you, I am sorry, Deborah, but —"

"You must forget last night, Simon. I have given this much thought. John's family befriended mine when we escaped from Caesarea. He needs me. We have been friends a long time, and we have come to understand each other and to want the same things."

"Then it is gratitude you owe him. Not love."

"You have no right to say these things! You presume too much!"

"But you love me! I know you do," I said, reaching for her.

"Do not touch me. You must not!" she whispered, backing away.

I could not lose her now. I could not! Facing each other, we were two wild creatures who screamed in agony without sound. "Oh, Deborah, Deborah, do not do this," I cried inwardly. But the words I spoke were cruel and bitter. "I am not sorry about last night. You lie if you say you do not care, or want me, as I want you. At least I am honest. You must not marry John. You would wrong him as well as me!"

The shofar blasted for the second time. I wanted to go, but had to stay. Deborah's lips trembled, and she looked away, listening until the summons ended.

Then, turning to me with a look of determination and pain that I can never forget, she said, "I love John, Simon. I do. I do. Please, do not hurt me more. Forget what happened last night. Forget me."

I swallowed the lump in my throat. "Forget? How?" I asked, miserable at the finality in her voice.

"You must, Simon," she said, reaching to comfort me, but withdrawing her hand suddenly, as if from a fire. "If you cannot, we cannot remain friends. And I could not bear that."

"Deborah!" I pleaded once more, hopelessly, as the shofar sounded the third time.

"We must go to the wall now," she said, already hurrying away. "There is no more to be said."

Chapter VIII

"Make camp," I commanded when our legion was yet a half-day's march from Masada. My words were echoed by each centurion in turn.

My eyes sought out the rock ahead, some three miles distant yet. I could imagine the figures of the defenders, like ants, swarming the ramparts to see our approach. That was good. Timing is all important. We could have reached the fortress this same day, but tomorrow would be better. It is a simple fact of warfare: Give the enemy a few hours of daylight to observe your strength, and the entire night in which to multiply that strength in imagination. Often, then, he thinks better of resistance.

Soon the familiar noise of organizing the campsite and getting settled for the coming night filled the air. The dust of activity finally settled, and in its place came the smoke of campfires, then the aroma of wild boar roasting on spits. Water may be hard to come by, with no near spring, but meat will be plentiful. These hills abound in game; our hunting parties have had no difficulty satisfying our needs.

55

Everywhere I walked that evening, I could feel the restrained excitement of our soldiers. The apathy of the last week was gone, the grueling two-week march already forgotten. Instead, men sang around the campfires late into the night, or went to the Sea of Salt to swim. They returned laughing, talking loudly about the amazing water that held them afloat even when they wished to sink. They called for the Jewish slaves to fetch fresh water for them, that they might wash off the brine that burned their skin. Finally, the centurions quieted the camp, and the legion began to settle for the night. Soon, except for the occasional snort of a horse, the distant laugh of a hyena, or the crackling of the campfires, silence came.

We broke camp shortly before sunrise the next day and were on our way before the sun rose over the mountains of Moab. Marius rode beside me, silent and morose, as was his way. He comes to life at night, alert long after sleep takes me. Where I am bright and hopeful in the morning, morning always finds him dull, capable only of grunts when spoken to. His quiet was a welcome thing to me, for I enjoyed the invigorating cool, the fresh earth smells, the bird calls, the brilliance of color as the sun climbed the sky.

Soon, though, Marius was himself again, the efficient senior centurion who had fought beside me through many a battle. I knew his humor had returned as soon as he called for drink. It was so every day. A servant would run up with a flask of wine. Marius would rinse his mouth, spit out the first mouthfuls, always to the left, then drink the flask-full almost without taking breath. His tongue would loosen then, as though the wine were a lubricant, and soon there would be no stopping him.

"Well, now," he began, in his usual contemptuous tone, "do you suppose any Zealots escaped during the night?" I sighed, reluctant to engage in this kind of duel so early in the day.

"I know the fortress well, Flavius. I visited there when the Roman garrison held it some years ago," he continued.

He had told me this many times before. I resigned myself to listen once again, for once started, Marius never needed prompting to continue.

"What luxury!" He shook his head in wonder. "That hanging palace Herod built is something to see. And that is not the only one. There is another on the summit, to the west. It must have been his ceremonial palace. There is even a throne room and a throne on a raised platform in one of the rooms. You must see the mosaic floor in the vestibule. So richly colored, laid out in intricate fruit designs. It rivals anything I have seen in Rome." He paused. "Did I ever tell you about the cisterns?"

"I have seen the layout of Masada in drawings made by the men who were garrisoned there," I said. "There are twelve, I believe."

"Yes. Now that is engineering genius for you!"

"Where does the water come from?" I asked.

"To the north and south of Masada are two clefts in the mountains. Herod's engineers built an aqueduct from the southern cleft, which is really just a dry riverbed most of the year, to the upper series of cisterns. The northern channel links up with the lower row of cisterns."

"Very interesting. But there is so little rain here. Surely an inch or so a year cannot amount to much in the cisterns."

"True," Marius said, always glad to teach me something. "But there are flash floods! The water comes from many miles away, usually from a sudden, heavy downpour. It rushes down the mountain slopes with great force and speed, and in huge volume, filling the dry riverbeds in seconds. A friend of mine drowned in such a flood while traveling with his men to join the legion at Petra. Suddenly the water gushed into the canyon so swiftly that it was over their heads before most of them could scramble to higher ground."

"Yes, I heard about that," I said. "Go on."

"Well, Herod harnessed these floods by building dams at the two clefts, and from these the aqueducts were constructed. They carried the floodwaters down the sloping hills and spilled them into the cisterns."

"I have seen the aqueduct that carries water from the mountains to Caesarea. It is forty miles long, so I am not surprised," I said.

Marius continued. Pride filled his voice. "You really must see the cisterns themselves, scooped out of the cliffside by hand. One of them is so huge, I wouldn't be surprised if it was, let me see — oh, at least twenty paces long by six wide and six high. And there are staircases in each, so you can descend as the water level drops. Those cisterns hold enough water to supply the Zealots until the next flash flood. If we can get to that supply — or block off the water flow somehow — they will die of thirst."

I considered this for a time. "The rainy season will be here soon. Perhaps we can destroy the aqueducts, but there will still be water in the cisterns from earlier rains."

"True," Marius agreed.

"However, there may be no need to capture the cisterns. Perhaps the Jews will surrender."

Marius looked my way with a strange expression on his face. He opened his mouth to speak, but seemed to change his mind. We trotted along awhile in silence, and then I said, "If they do not surrender, we must take them quickly. It will not look well in Rome should such a small band of fanatics hold up the entire Tenth Legion."

Just before midday, we reached the foot of Masada. Even knowing the dimensions of the rock does not prepare one for the sight. Coming from the north, as we did, the mountain seems impossibly steep. How Herod could have brought the building materials to the top of this high rock in itself is a thing of wonder. That his engineers could have carved the step-shaped palace that hangs from the north face without a loss of many lives is inconceivable. The wall at the top gleams brightly. Could it be of marble?

I directed the legion to proceed round the base of the mountain, an operation that took most of the remaining daylight hours. In a way, this is a theatrical display in which all our men take part. The foot soldiers, with their metal helmets and shields reflecting the sun, march with greater spirit. The cavalry rides a little straighter. The standard bearers strut with self-conscious pride. The trumpeters sound their orders with greater power, clearer tones. A larger distance forms between the men and the machines, so that the quick-loaders, the stone-throwing catapults, and the battering rams stand out more clearly as the most lethal weapons to fear. There is nothing that terrifies an enemy more than this dramatic show of strength.

When we had encircled the rock, a distance of perhaps three miles, our forces halted and at my command faced inward. Then, after a long moment of silence, with each man's face turned upward toward the rock, I gave the signal. Whether foot soldier or cavalry, each raised his sword or spear in simultaneous action, uttering at the same instant a loud and terrifying shout. To this day I remember the thrill I felt at the unity, the strength, the discipline, the spirit of my men.

I nodded to Marius, who knew my meaning instantly. He turned his horse toward the Jewish prisoners, returning soon, leading a ragged-looking older man with hands tied before him. A rope connected his wrists to Marius's saddle. The man struggled valiantly to keep up with the horse's pace.

"Does he understand what he is to do?" I asked Marius. The man stood puffing and red-faced before me. Perspiration ran in rivulets down his dusty face.

"No, I have not told him," he replied.

"Untie him first," I said, "and give him water." I watched while the man drank, his hands trembling violently. Marius looked away, eyes fixed upon a distant point, yet he gripped his whip with a fierceness that belied his calm.

I turned to the prisoner. His breath came more steadily now. With downcast eyes, he muttered his gratitude.

"Your name?"

"Ananias," he replied quietly.

"Ananias. You will repeat after me, in the language of the Jews, whatever you hear me say. Do you understand?" I asked.

He nodded.

"Do you understand?" I demanded. "And you will look at me!"

He raised his gaze slowly, and for a moment we took each other's measure. His face was gaunt, his body limp with fatigue. Hollows showed in his cheeks. "I understand," he said at last, and in his eyes was both such vengeance and such despair that I turned away.

I moved my horse to a position where I stood apart from my men. Ananias followed. "Tell them who speaks," I commanded.

60

Ananias's voice rang clearly in the air, echoing off the nearby hills as he spoke in the strange tongue of the Jews. Then he stepped back and waited for me to continue.

I did not need to shout, for sound carries here as it would in a tunnel.

"You are surrounded. Judea has fallen. Jerusalem has been destroyed. Surrender now, or die!"

Even before Ananias could begin the translation, there came a stirring from above. We could not see them from that angle, but they must have stood shoulder to shoulder atop the wall. Suddenly an avalanche of rocks came tumbling down the sides of the mountain, jumping, skipping, gathering momentum, raising dust and dislodging other rocks. My horse reared and whinnied. Our soldiers, shouting and screaming, pushed back frantically to escape the oncoming mass of rubble.

Above the thunder of rocks falling and horses neighing in panic, I could hear laughter from above, wild and jubilant.

Suddenly I remembered Marius's words. "They do not deserve the chance to surrender!" he had said. I did not want to see his face now, knowing I would strike its look of triumph. While part of me admired the fearless tactic, any compassion I had felt for these Jews shriveled within me in that moment. If the Jews wanted war, they would get it. In full. Without mercy. Till their last man was dead!

Chapter IX

There was but one thing to do. Attack! At once! Before the enemy could savor its advantage, before our troops could feel the shame I felt already.

"Archers — fire!" I shouted above the din. My horse struggled to regain his balance. The dust from falling rocks rose to the stallion's knees. Immediately the trumpeters picked up my order and broadcast it down the line of troops. Instantly the first arrows shot upward, curving toward the walled fortress. Again and again the arrows flew, stinging the air like angry bees. Many fell short, but many also found their mark, for the cries of wounded Jews could be heard all along the wall above. But still the rocks rained down.

When finally the onslaught slowed, my eyes swept the nearby troops, assessing damage. They had stood the attack well. Already they were reforming ranks, awaiting further orders. Reports came in of minor losses: one man dead, his skull crushed; two horses with broken legs; a dozen or so men with inconsequential injuries; a few prisoners trampled to death by frantic horses.

Suddenly I remembered the prisoner Ananias. Where was he now? I looked among the men nearby. He was not there. I galloped to the spot where we had stood when the hail of rocks began to fall. The dust was still thick, but settling now. And there he stood, one hand grasping a bleeding arm, his head turned up toward the walls of the fortress. And most strange: he smiled! And his eyes — they beheld Masada with a joy, a rapture I cannot describe. Was he mad? Or was this the face of all the Zealots on that rock? Were they too madmen, burning with the lust of self-destruction?

Marius trotted up and followed my grim look to the prisoner. Mistaking my perplexity for hatred, he saw us allied now for revenge. Smiling as though we shared some private joke, he kneed his horse and, leaning forward, raced at the prisoner, barely missing the bent figure. Then, turning swiftly, he galloped back, unfurling his whip as he went and slicing the air with sharp, clear cracks. The prisoner crouched in terror, hands covering his face, as man and horse bore down on him. Then, with a laugh, Marius struck. The whip flicked out like a serpent's tongue, meeting the prisoner's back and leaving behind a long wound, gushing blood.

"That is what we will do to your friends up there!" he shouted so those on the rock might hear. And from our ranks came encouraging shouts and laughter.

How pointless! Yet I did not intercede. I sat stiffly, barely controlling my contempt, yet permitting this revolting act of cowardice for two good reasons. I had been shamed before my men when my appeal for peace was met by violence. By sanctioning this cruelty now, I regained face and stood avenged. The second reason was yet more important. I knew the restless urge to fight my men had nurtured these last weeks. Tensed and eager to engage the Jews in battle, they came to find the enemy out of reach, even out of sight, and themselves in a vulnerable position. This gave my men an outlet — a moment of brutality that relieved the helplessness they felt and did not understand.

Again I wish to note: Marius is one to watch. Military acts must be deliberate and well thought out, never without purpose. Marius acts impulsively, not figuring the consequences. This time his abhorrent behavior worked in my favor, but he did not think before he acted; that is always dangerous.

I set up camp on the west, where the land falls less sharply from the rock. Marius sent for our engineers, and by evening we met to exchange information.

"We have circled the rock twice, General, and it is clear what we must do," the spokesman for the engineers said, smoothing out a map upon the table in my tent.

"There are only two places the Jews might escape. Here and here." He pointed to the east and to the west.

"The snake-path route is noisy and slow. They would announce their coming long before they reached the bottom, for they could not fail to dislodge rocks and earth as they crept down. Still, some could escape that way. We should build a large camp at the base there," the engineer recommended, "and at least one smaller camp nearby. A second large camp should be built just north of where we are now. That would put you, Commander, in the best position to observe any escape down the western slope. Escape from north or south is virtually impossible, but we should build small camps there nevertheless."

"If we encircle them with a wall, we can prevent escape and keep reinforcements from reaching them," I said. "Is such a circumvallation wall practicable?"

"I think so," the engineer answered. "But it would take time and considerable manpower."

"We have both."

"Roughly, such a wall would stretch over two miles. If you wish us to build it, I would recommend several towers be incorporated on the east side particularly, the snake-path side."

"At least six towers in all," one of the others interjected, "for there is a broad area to oversee."

The spokesman nodded. "Yes, that is so. And we feel the smaller camps could be integral with the wall, saving time in building and putting them closer to trouble spots."

"In all, how many camps do you plan?" I asked.

The engineers conferred briefly. Then the first said, "We have not settled on that yet. Perhaps eight, with most of the legion garrisoned in the largest two."

Such quick assessment of the requirements for a siege takes a practiced eye and vast experience. "You have done well for so short a time," I said, genuinely impressed, "but it was not only encirclement I had in mind. It is not my wish to sit below and wait for the Jews to starve or die of thirst. I want to *claim* that summit. I want to personally inform Vespasian that the last resistance in Judea has been quelled!"

For a while, all were silent, studying the map.

Marius, a cup of wine in hand, asked, "What of a siege ramp? We cannot use our machines from this low position."

"Yes, a ramp will be necessary. And not too difficult to build," the spokesman replied. "The drop on the west could be no more than five hundred feet. We can bring it up to half that distance from the summit, then construct a platform from which our machines can operate. There is no great problem there. Only a question of time."

"How long?" I asked.

The engineer looked to his associates. They shrugged.

"How long?" I asked again, annoyed at their uncertainty.

They gathered over the map and talked together of numbers of Jewish prisoners, of earth to be moved, of rocks to be positioned, and of lumber needed. "Ten months." The spokesman hesitated. "Perhaps less. Depends on how much the Jews harass the operations."

"Too long," I stated flatly. "Two years ago Vespasian issued 'Judea Capta' coins commemorating the victory here. Until Masada falls, Judea is not officially ours."

"As for harassment by the Zealots, do not worry," Marius added. "We will see that they do not impede your construction."

The engineer nodded. "Then six to eight months."

"It is now September. I wish to be back in Caesarea by February, March at the very latest," I insisted.

"We will do our best," the spokesman said.

They were true to their word. By the first light of morning, everyone was at work. While the Jewish prisoners began the arduous task of mining rocks, the engineers made a detailed survey of the terrain. Within the week, they established the position of eight camps, and marked the line of the circumvallation wall at such a distance from the base of Masada that rocks hurled down by the defenders would be of little disturbance. Within the month, our two large camps on the east and west and the six smaller ones were well underway, and those of the prisoners were spread out nearby. By the end of October, the circumvallation wall was completed.

The Zealots on Masada were as sealed in as they

thought us sealed out. Every possible escape route was guarded. One camp barred passage through Wadi Sebbeth; another closed the exit from Wadi Nimrein; another guarded the beginning stretch of the snake path. One camp was situated atop the rock south of Wadi Sebbeth, opposite the southern edge of Masada, looking down upon the summit of the fortress. The small camp nearest mine would guard my camp and prevent the Zealots from reaching their cisterns.

Because of the expected length of our stay, our camps were more permanently constructed than usual, with stone walls forming a large rectangle. In the large camps, two main roads bisected the rectangle, north to south and east to west, allowing for speedy egress through the gates in each of the four walls in the event of attack.

My command post had a large central court with a dining hall where twelve people could comfortably take meals, seated on the stone couches along the sides. There were places of worship, a platform from which I could address the troops, altars for the Legion's sacrifices, marketplaces, a treasury — even an observatory from which our camp priests could watch the flight of birds or view the stars in order to predict the optimum times for attack. The troops were quartered eight to nine men to a tent, sleeping on stone benches therein.

Now we could concentrate on completing the ramp.

MARIUS PROVED TO BE an exacting taskmaster. The Jewish slaves worked dawn to dusk, with a brief rest at the height of the day, when even the lizards sought shelter from the sun. Many collapsed from heat and exhaustion and were dragged out of the way by the soldiers who directed the work. Several centuries and a large number of prisoners went north to bring back cedar and other lumber from what forests still remained. One entire cohort took water duty, on rotation. With the nearest spring many miles away, keeping the camp supplied adequately with water for drinking, for washing, and for the horses became the task of the Jewish prisoners, who did most of the carrying.

The days of preparation for the siege were long, hot, and dusty. I spent them riding along the line of the circumvallation wall, checking the progress and urging greater speed. The rains came late that year, making the long dry season seem endless. Coming as I do from the north of our empire, I am used to greater moisture. The dust seemed to invade my nostrils and never leave. My skin crawled from the dryness, though I took to oiling it finally. My nose bled suddenly and profusely at unpredictable times, causing me great distress. I took comfort in knowing that the Jews suffered from the drought almost as much as we. Each day without rain meant less water in the cisterns above. We had dammed up the aqueducts leading to their hillside cisterns so that if rain came, none would flow into them. Eventually, we knew, the Jews must replenish their water supply from those cisterns, and when they did, we would be waiting.

During those weeks, I took to riding regularly through the prisoners' camps, seeking to understand what drives these people to such fanatic resolve. Marius could not understand my purpose. "They will take it as a weakness," he argued, his eyes narrowing with suspicion. "That the Commander of the great Tenth Legion should go among such lowly scum will be misunderstood. They will look for favors. They will appeal to your sympathies and demand better conditions. You will see," he said prophetically. "What is your purpose?"

"There is something about these people that I must

understand," I said. "What makes them resist us when the outcome is so clear? There are women and children above. Have they no heart for their survival? Why do they fight against such odds? I have never met such an enemy."

Marius studied me closely, intrigued for a moment by this incongruity.

"I will go with you," he offered, "but not for your reason. There are more than a few comely women among these prisoners. I should like to see them at their cooking pots. They might prove better companions in the night than the camp harlots I have had."

Two trips I made with Marius to the prisoners' camps, and details of these I herein record. In setting down the sights and smells and vague impressions, I may find some meaning that escapes me still.

When first we visited, we entered unannounced at night, riding slowly and silently through their streets. I noticed none of the organization typical of our camps. Tents leaned against tents; many slept outdoors. Cooking pots in central areas smelled of barley gruel and garlic.

Most of all I was struck by the atmosphere. Remember now that these prisoners were for the most part unrelated, having been taken from fortresses in Galilee, Jerusalem, Sepphoris, and other cities. The old and very young had been killed on the spot, being of no value to us. The strong young men had been sent to the mines — or the arenas; the girls of beauty and children sold as slaves. Like lengths of cloth, families had been torn to shreds. Yet for all this, these poor remnants of other lives, with few ties of blood, lived here as family. Women cooked for the men and tended the children. At our approach, the men stepped protectively in front of them.

Tired though they must have been after the long, hard

day in the sun, they were nevertheless clean, with faces washed of the day's dirt and hair neatly combed. Men sat outside their tents reading the strange Hebrew script to the children, but when we approached, they hastily rolled up the scrolls.

"You wish to understand these people?" Marius whispered fiercely. "Watch!" Reining his horse, he dismounted and approached a Jew who held a scroll. "Give it to me," he commanded in Aramaic. The prisoner backed away, hiding the scroll behind him. Marius touched his sword. Reluctantly the man proffered the scroll. Marius glanced casually at the carefully lettered parchment. Then, watching the prisoner's face, he drew his sword and slashed it to shreds, its pieces flying off in the wind.

The horror on the faces of those close by amazed me. After all, it was but a scroll! Of what significance? There must be others. Yet children cried and rushed to snatch up the falling pieces.

"It is part of their book of laws," Marius said, remounting his horse, as if that explained everything. Yet what did it explain? Even now, as I try to understand the Jews' reactions, the real meaning eludes me.

Our coming brought fear, for as word of our presence spread, the streets quickly emptied. Before our eyes, tent flaps closed. Except for one. In the center of the camp we came upon Ananias, standing, arms folded, eyes challenging, before his tent. The wounds of his recent lashing had not yet healed. As we approached, he regarded Marius with deliberate scorn, and as we passed, I felt sure he watched us till we left the gates.

Ananias's contempt had been lost on Marius, it seemed, for as we returned to camp, he said with obvious relish, "Did you see that woman in his tent?"

"What woman?" I asked, for I had seen only Ananias.

"You did not see her?" he asked, surprised. "That prisoner? I forget his name — the one who addressed the Jews above. In his tent? A beauty! Long, dark hair, fair skin, and . . ." His eyes rolled heavenward. "Strange. I have not seen her working on the wall. I must watch for her," he said.

After that evening, they must have stationed a lookout, for on our second visit, it was as if we entered a dead city. Not a single person walked the streets. Cooking pots simmered unattended. And though the night was hot, each tent flap was firmly closed. Again we found Ananias outside his tent, arms crossed over his chest. When we drew abreast, he spoke with insolence, and I found it difficult to control my anger.

"What evil mission brings you here this time? Is it not enough that we are your prisoners? What more do you want?" he demanded.

"Hold your tongue, Jew, or you will know the consequences." Ananias bowed his head. In a softer tone, I said, "Tell me about your people on Masada," I said.

He searched my face a moment, then motioned for us to enter his tent. I dismounted and entered the poor tent with Marius, leaving my guards at rest outside.

There was little within: straw mats for sleeping, a few kitchen implements, an oil lamp, a small bundle of clothes in a corner. In another corner, two children huddled close to a young woman with a zither in her lap. Was this the woman Marius had seen before? It hardly seemed likely. Her fair face was marked with dirt, her body clothed in a sack that concealed her shape. And the long, dark hair Marius had admired was a rough stubble on a nearly bald pate. Marius's obvious distaste and shock at the sight of her made me laugh. Yet the girl was a beauty! In the moment she had looked up at our entrance, I saw gray-

71

green eyes with intelligence and defiance. Seating myself on a mat facing Ananias, I realized that they were the same eyes as his, only her brother's eyes showed scorn, stubbornness, and pride as well.

Marius sat with us, darting quick glances at the girl. He seemed puzzled and uncomfortable. Of course! On our first visit, the Jew had recognized Marius's lustful glance at his sister. How many other of the women here were also shorn of their hair, deliberately dirty of face, draped with shapeless garments so as not to appeal to our soldiers.

"I cannot offer you food or drink," Ananias said. "As you well know, we have barely enough to survive ourselves." Marius gave me a quick look as if to say, "I told you he would ask for favors."

"What is it you wish to know?"

"Why do the Jews of Masada resist? I would like to understand. I would truly like to know."

"They prefer freedom to slavery," he said after a pause.

"Ridiculous!" I snarled. "If that were so, why did they not resist when Rome first claimed Judea as a province, more than a hundred years ago? Why now, when it is too late?"

Ananias shrugged. "I cannot speak for my people's decisions a hundred years ago. Only now. Freedom cannot be sold, bit by bit, to buy peace. The cost is too high. And eventually there is nothing more to sell."

"But they have been given a chance to surrender! By refusing, they virtually sign their death warrants! Is life so cheap then?"

He laughed mirthlessly. "*You* speak of life being cheap! What value do *you* put on it? Where is your mercy? Where is your love of man? How many men, women, and

72

children have you cut down, without a thought, as easily as discarding chaff? And *nobly*, in the name of conquest!"

"Unfortunate, but such is the price the defeated must pay. It has been so throughout history," I said.

"Does that make it right? Or moral? Can any empire survive which counts life of such little worth? Will you kill everyone who thinks differently from you? Him also — if he goes against your orders?" He pointed to Marius.

Marius turned scarlet and looked ready to strike the prisoner. I raised my hand to stave him off. Then, infuriated myself at this man's insolence, I lost patience.

"I did not come to argue ways of life with you! I thought you might want to try to save those on Masada. You may not believe me, but I would prefer to end this siege now, without bloodshed. If you know a way to do this, you may yet save many."

Ananias smirked knowingly. "It is not compassion or pity you feel! It is fear! You cannot reach them on that rock. That is why you appeal to me! And I will help you no more!"

He seemed to understand something. "You have lost already! For even if you should reach them, the Jews of Masada will fight you to the last man. What will Vespasian say then!"

I leaped to my feet and struck him violently. The young woman gasped, and the children began to weep. Ananias held his hand to his cheek. His eyes flashed with hatred.

"Would that I could be up there with them — fighting you. But I am a coward," he whispered bitterly, "a traitor. I build your wall, against my own bethren. I do your evil bidding. Why? To live another day."

Chapter X

They are like ants, those Romans! Three weeks have passed since their arrival, and every day has been the same. They scurry over the desert floor, this way and that, and gradually, the landscape takes on a new shape. From slits in the outer wall and from the towers, we can see it all. Patrols leave early in the morning and return at night, sometimes with lumber, occasionally with game, frequently with heavy jugs that must contain water. Large numbers of ill-clad prisoners scrape at the terrain, mining rocks, moving mountains of boulders that gradually disappear into the rectangles of their camps or the immense wall they are building around our base.

From this height we cannot make out faces. I wonder if any of those prisoners are former friends? It hurts to see them work so diligently toward our destruction.

Yet, were I in their place, what would I do?

Strange, how quickly one adjusts to anything. The first day that construction began, the sound was terrible. I could not hear anything else. Every blow of pick on rock resounded doubly in the clear air, and was like a blow struck at me.

And it is not that I am more sensitive than others. Our people walked quietly, talked in whispers, listened intently.

How strange that seems now that I am used to the noise. Within a few days those sounds became as ordinary to our ears as the whistling of the wind that blows from the south. If they had ceased suddenly, we would have all become alarmed.

For most people, life returned nearly to normal. We could take little aggressive action against the Romans, for our rocks and arrows fell short of their camps. And so we watched and waited.

I now spent mornings with Ananus ben Ezra, and in the first weeks I learned much about tending wounds. Several of our people had been struck by arrows that first day, and the physician showed me how to cleanse a wound, treat it with salve, and bind it. Gradually he introduced me to the many herbs he stored, and even demonstrated how to mix certain preparations for infections of the eye.

I found it more painful to join Deborah and John, as I had before, than to avoid them altogether. I could not be near her without aching to say what was in my heart. And the warmth I had once felt for John had cooled. Having betrayed our friendship by avowing my love to Deborah, and knowing I would do so again if given the chance, made me uncomfortable in his presence. Instead, I took to spending my spare time at Ananus ben Ezra's home, even to taking meals with him.

The physician was a man of good humor and much wisdom. I know now that he must have recognized my unhappiness, for he gave me much of his spare time. His wife accepted my presence naturally, and his daughter, Salome, looked forward to my coming, her round, kind face turning pink at my approach and deep red whenever she had to serve me. She had her mother's generous figure and her father's twinkling eyes, and a shyness both sweet and childlike. Her attention was flattering, but it did little to ease my longing for Deborah.

In the fifth week of the siege, my father announced publicly that my brother Aram would be married to Sara the following week, two days before Erev Shabbat. The entire community was invited to the wedding.

The news gave us something happy to think about, something hopeful. When I allowed myself to speculate about the ominous activity below, progressing methodically, day after day, the vision of the end result became intolerable. Only by pushing these thoughts aside, by becoming immersed in activity of any kind, could I live with it. The upcoming wedding offered just such an opportunity. Preparing for it and looking forward to it almost made it possible to pretend the Romans below were no real threat. Some even reasoned, If Eleazar's son is to be wed, does that not mean Eleazar has confidence in a future?

The rationing system I had recently put into effect was relaxed somewhat to prepare for the feast. Though the flour, oil, honey, and wines were double those issued for a normal week's rations, it seemed justified, under the circumstances.

As soon as the news circulated, my father called a meeting of his captains. When we had all gathered in the room behind the synagogue, he said, "We will refill the cisterns above on Sabbath eve, two nights after the wedding."

He waited for his words to take effect. I stiffened.

Murmurs of surprise and disapproval came from many. Rabbi Hillel, seated near my father, frowned. "Can we not wait until after the Sabbath — or even the wedding night?" he implored. It was clear he had been over this ground already with my father, because Eleazer answered kindly but firmly, "I know your feelings, Rabbi, but this is war. God will understand. We must use every resource at our command, even to fighting on the Sabbath. On the wedding night, the Romans will be more alert for a surprise move, because of the unusual sounds. By Friday evening, they will have become accustomed to the noises of our celebrants. Besides, they will think, 'Surely the Jews would not attack on their day of rest and prayer!'"

The rabbi nodded, understanding but not accepting. The creases in his forehead grew deeper, and he fingered the fringe on his tallith.

John spoke up, his eyes bright. "It will be dark that night — with only a quarter moon. Why not combine the trip for water with a surprise attack? I could take thirty to forty men with me."

Rabbi Hillel's angry voice rang out. "Working on the Sabbath is bad enough. We need water! But killing on God's day? Unforgivable!"

My father ignored his outburst. "I do not know," he said slowly. "Even in daylight it is a long walk down the snake path. By night, with water jugs to carry, it would take longer. There is also the danger that the water carriers might accidentally block the path for your return, in the event you are pursued."

John held up a finger. "No danger of that! We go down first with our patrol to make sure the cisterns are still in our hands. Then the carriers start down. Say you send 150 men as soon as it is dark. They could make several trips. On the last, my patrol continues on down to the

Roman camp. The water carriers would be safe on the plateau long before we start back."

"I do not know," my father repeated, pulling at his beard. "Is it worth the risk to the water bearers?"

"Are we to just do nothing, then?" John asked, incredulous. "Wait for them to come to us? What have we to lose?"

"It will be a thin moon," someone offered hopefully.

"And the paths are clear of obstructions," Aram added. "We have had patrols out all week clearing both the snake path and the cistern path, so we might use them more safely in just such an operation. There is far less danger of stumbling, or of rocks falling to alert the Romans . . ."

My father looked beyond us, considering carefully. Then, clapping his hands together suddenly, he said, "I have been thinking like an old man, too cautiously. Yes, why not! We will do it!"

"Then it is set," Aram said with finality, "for the second night after my wedding."

"There is no need for you to go, Aram," I objected. "We will have enough men without you. Besides, Sara . . ." I broke off.

Aram dismissed my protest with a casual shrug. "Sara will understand, and forgive," he said with certainty.

Then, as though some terrible thought had crossed his mind, a stricken look came over his face. "The huppah! I must build one for our wedding, or Sara might not marry me!" We all laughed, delighted by his deliberately pitiful expression.

"On your feet, everyone!" I cried, feeling some of the joy Aram carried with him lately. "We had better get to work and help this poor lout. Sara must not be married without a huppah over her head!"

Chapter XI

Constructing the huppah, the canopy symbolic of the groom's house, was a joyful experience. Despite our recent discomfort with each other, John and I joined Aram and his best friends to make the most beautiful huppah ever built on Masada. With wood we stripped from the roof structures of Herod's palace, we raised the frame of the huppah. While we worked, we forgot for a time the outside world and spoke instead of experiences we had shared. Aram told us again how he had come to notice Sara.

"I saw her the first time we went to Ein Gedi for palm fronds," he said as he knocked a nail into a support. "We were all supposed to stay close together, because of wild animals. Only the men carried weapons, remember? Well, somehow, when we found the waterfall, everyone dispersed. John, you and Simon ducked under the falls, laughing and trying to drink the water at the same time. You looked like you were drowning! A few of the girls sat together, pointing and giggling. For no particular reason, I decided to climb above the falls and look around."

At this point in his story, my mother came out of our apartment, carrying a small bowl of figs, which we consumed almost as quickly as they appeared. Since rationing began, we no longer enjoyed delicacies between meals. As I slowly bit into the plump, rich fruit, letting the seeds rest on my tongue for a long time before swallowing, I idly wondered how my mother had come by this treat. When I looked at her more closely, I knew. Her tall, stately body looked gaunt. Her dress hung loosely, as though it belonged to another. How often had she saved her portion of the ration in order to give it to us later?

"Mother," I began. She turned her tired eyes in my direction and gave me a warm smile, a look I had not seen in many months. "Yes, Simon?"

I could not spoil her pleasure now. "Nothing," I replied, kissing her on the forehead, "except that you are beautiful."

We turned back to Aram, who went on with his story. "Above the falls, I became aware of a movement behind some palm trees in a small clearing. I thought it might be an animal, and I approached quietly, drawing an arrow and setting it in my bow."

"An animal?" John inquired, knowing the answer from previous tellings.

Aram grinned with pleasure at the memory of it. "Indeed! It was Sara. Thinking herself alone in the clearing, she was dancing, waving a palm frond." He laughed. "She was singing a song from Solomon — about the Shulammite, I think — and looked so graceful, so incredibly beautiful, that I wondered why I had not noticed her before. Just then, I heard another sound directly behind her: the snort of a boar. But Sara was so lost in her dance that she was unaware of the danger. I could hide myself no longer. I burst into the clearing, pushing her out of the way, and shot the boar. And do you know what thanks I got?"

We all looked up from our work on the huppah, awaiting his answer. My mother smiled tenderly.

"Sara glanced at the dead animal as if it meant nothing to her. Then she glared at me with those fierce brown eyes of hers and said, 'Aram ben Eleazar. You were following me!' Can you imagine!"

"Then what?" I prodded, always enjoying the end of this story.

"Then," Aram said proudly, "she turned on her heel, gathered up a half-dozen palm fronds, and with her head in the air marched off down the path without another word. How's that for spirit!"

We agreed that he was a very fortunate man and urged him to tell more stories. My mother rose and left the room but soon returned with an armful of white linen, embroidered in gold and purple, sewn long ago for her own marriage. On the wedding day, this would become the roof of the huppah.

Since learning of the wedding, I had pondered what gift to choose for Sara and my brother. I wanted it to be very special. I visited the tannery, where I saw many fine leather goods, but nothing appropriate for a wedding gift. Our weavers no longer wove fine cloth. Pottery was even more disappointing, for the wares were all of fired clay, practical but of no true beauty. The few bronze pieces also were too utilitarian.

"I have shekels to pay for a gift," I lamented to Ananus ben Ezra one day, "but there just doesn't seem to be anything for sale. Money means nothing here, since we all share equally now in what is left. No one bothers to produce things of beauty anymore, only things for survival."

With sadness the physician agreed. "That is true. The only beautiful things we have are left from the days before the war."

"But no one wants to part with them," I said. "They are not for sale."

Salome had been listening, and now she came to stand near her father's chair. The physician put a thin arm around his daughter and smiled up at her. "Now here is a thing of loveliness that remains from the old days," he said lovingly.

Salome blushed, and her eyes would not meet mine. In spite of that, she said, "I know of a gift you might give."

"What, Salome?"

"It is a vase of alabaster, cool to the touch, so fine the sunlight shows through it, so graceful in shape it is — I mean, your hand wants to follow its curve." It was the longest speech she had ever made to me. When she was through, she looked up with her big, bright, innocent eyes and smiled shyly. For the first time, I saw her as a woman.

Ananus ben Ezra had been watching his daughter with a strange, quizzical look. Suddenly he nodded his head in understanding.

"Where is this vase, Salome?" I asked eagerly. "It sounds like the very thing I have been seeking."

"It may not be for sale," she said.

"I do not understand. Then why did you tell me of it?"

"Remember the ailing mother whose daughter brought her here the first day you came to work with my father?"

I nodded.

"She owns the vase. When she fled Jerusalem, she

82

brought it with her against her daughter's wishes. Her daughter argued that the vase was large and heavy. The precious space it took would be better filled by things of practical value. The daughter still chides her mother about her foolishness."

"Do you think she might sell it, considering she puts such value on it?" I asked, full of hope.

"I do not know. We can only ask."

WHEN WE ENTERED the tiny room that had been built against the casemate wall with materials from Herod's palace, my eye immediately caught sight of the vase Salome had described. It rested on a marble slab, part of a pillar from the palace, I suppose, near the mother's bed. It was filled with dried leaves in shades of red and gold. The smoothness of the milk-hued alabaster contrasted with the withered leaves and made me think of the difference between the skin of Salome and that of the old woman.

Miriamme, the woman's daughter, stirred the contents of a cooking pot and barely acknowledged our greeting. I addressed myself to the mother, asking after her health and telling her, finally, about my quest for a gift for Sara and my brother. "Would you sell me this vase, dear mother?"

She smiled a toothless smile and in a dry voice said, "Sara is a good girl. She has often come to visit and to sing to me."

The daughter became suddenly alert. "How can one prepare decent food with what you permit us in rations!"

"It is not easy," Salome agreed sympathetically. "My mother also complains, but rationing is necessary."

The daughter wiped her hands on a cloth. Her eyes

regarded us shrewdly. "I would wager *your* cooking pots hold more than mine!"

"That is not so!" I said, my voice rising.

"Ha!" she challenged.

"Miriamme, Miriamme," the old woman's voice protested sadly.

The daughter regarded her mother contemptuously. "If you had not insisted on bringing that vase and all those other useless things of your past, we would have more to eat now!"

The younger woman turned to us. "You want my mother's vase? Give us one month's additional rations."

I was so surprised, I could not speak.

"No one need know," she continued. She turned to her mother again. "Look at her, wasting away for lack of proper food, when the supply rooms are full. To issue extra food to two old women — in the end, what difference could it make?"

"I could not do that," I said coldly. "You are wicked to suggest I might. It would be stealing from the rest." Salome stood rigid, eyes on Miriamme. I felt suddenly tired. There were always some who could not believe in the decency or honesty of others. The rationing system applied to all, regardless of age or position, and was not so strict that a family might suffer.

"We must go, Salome," I said, turning to the door.

"Wait!" the mother called. She seemed to draw her withered body together. In a firm voice that left no room for argument, she said, "It is my vase, Miriamme! Not yours." She ran a hand lovingly over the smooth, milky surface of the vase. "Give it to them, please," she said, and held it out to Miriamme. "You have always taunted me for bringing this here. Let Sara and Aram enjoy its beauty. Maybe there will be peace between us when it is gone."

Salome tenderly kissed the old woman's forehead. The mother's eyes filled with tears. "It was a gift from my husband on our wedding day," she said.

Miriamme followed us from the room. I felt sorry for this woman who had lost her husband and children and now lived in resentment with her aged mother. She could not understand her mother's love for an object given her in love, nor the reason she could now so easily give away this object. Money was Miriamme's only security, I realized. Reaching into my pocket, I withdrew not one but two silver shekels and held them out to her. She took them eagerly, thanking us again and again as she turned them over in her hands.

"'Jerusalem the Holy. Silver Shekel,'" she read with growing excitement. "'Year four and Year five,'" she exclaimed in a voice that could be heard many meters away, drawing bystanders to her side.

I understood her wonder. The coins were struck in the fourth and fifth years of our revolt against the Romans. None had been minted since. Even she had recognized the importance of what she held in her hand. Those silver shekels probably represented the last coins our people would ever strike in Judea — unless by some miracle we would someday, once again, become a nation.

Chapter XII

A ram's wedding day dawned hot and humid. The winds brought sand from the south and pushed black clouds swiftly across the sky. The clouds were the first signs of winter rain, but the sun shone around and through them, and by noon the winds had driven them to the north.

Rather than go to Ananus ben Ezra's office that morning, I restlessly walked the ramparts, making my way around the wall, stopping occasionally to peer through the slits at the activity below. The Roman wall progressed well, and though it was comforting to know it separated us from the enemy, it was disquieting to realize that soon our escape routes would all be sealed off.

I planned on going to the bath house before dressing, but went first to the hanging palace, feeling a melancholy that was difficult to define, much less dispel. The voices of laughing children rose from one of the rooms on the upper terrace, and when I entered the room to see what caused the gaiety, I found them playing on the mosaic floor. A child tossed a pebble into one of the hexagons that patterned the floor, hopped into the space, and then kicked the pebble into the next hexagon. All the while, his friends tried to spoil his turn by teasing and chiding.

How easily children find diversion! Would that this were true of adults. And then it came to me why I felt so mournful on this day of joy. Today, Aram, younger than I by two years, would marry Sara. John, also younger than I, was now betrothed to Deborah. And I, a man of seventeen, the age for marriage, not only had no such plans but found no woman desirable other than one already spoken for. Envy and self-pity surged through me — and shame, that I could harbor such dark emotions.

I forced these thoughts from my mind and went directly to the bath house. The court was especially crowded because of the wedding. Usually I visited the tepidarium first, luxuriating in its comforting warmth while enjoying the beauty of the wall paintings. But this day, knowing so many awaited their turns to bathe, I passed through the room quickly and entered the caldarium. The water level had dropped, for now that it was increasingly dangerous to visit the cisterns, we replenished the bath-house waters, a luxury, last.

Bathed and dressed, I felt refreshed and optimistic. Good things baking in the many ovens for the wedding feast, and the cheerful faces of our people as they brought gifts to my parents' rooms or borrowed finery from each other, did much to help. I glimpsed Deborah entering the bride's apartment, already dressed for the wedding. The embroidered linen dress she wore brought out the rich olive tones of her skin, and her dark hair was braided and laced with ribbons. Her beauty made my heart ache.

In our apartment, my father was assigning guard duty, doubling the number of lookouts but shortening their time on watch so that each could participate in the wedding festivities. I drew the mid-evening shift on the western wall. John's watch would follow mine.

"Be especially alert," my father warned. "The Romans may think our merry-making good cover for attack. I pray they will not, but be sure the wedding activities do not divert you from your duties!"

Aram could not decide on a tunic. My mother gave me a despairing look. "Humor him," she whispered. "He is frantic with worry."

"What do you think?" Aram asked when he saw me. "Is this brown tunic right? Maybe I should wear the white one! And what about these sandals? They are so worn! Might I wear yours, Simon?"

While we exchanged sandals, I tried to reassure him that he made a handsome groom, no matter what he wore.

When he could get me alone, he asked, "What do you think? Is it too late to back out? Perhaps I am too young for the responsibilities of marriage!" His eyes grew large with excitement and fear.

"Perhaps," I agreed.

"What should I do?" he begged.

"Call off the wedding."

"Now? But the people have been invited! The preparations have been made! And Sara would die of shame!"

"Then marry her."

"But what do I know of marriage? Sara is a stranger. What will she be like in — fifty years? How do I know I will care for her then? Marriage is for such a long time! A lifetime!"

How optimistic love made him. Fifty years indeed! Just weeks ago he doubted we could hold the Romans off for five months. I sighed and looked at the ceiling. "Do you love Sara?" I asked.

"Yes. No. I thought I did — yesterday. But marriage!"

"Well, here is my solution," I said. "Do not call off the wedding. And you will not have to marry Sara, either."

"What?" he asked, alarmed by the sudden alternative.

"If you do not marry Sara today, *I* will."

At first Aram did not comprehend, but as he recognized the trap I had set, he laughed and laughed till tears streaked his face. Then he hugged me. At last, arm in arm, we left the rooms and with his friends went out to meet the bride.

The bridal procession moved slowly toward us across the plateau of Masada. Surely the sounds of singing, of laughter, of musical instruments could be heard across the Sea of Salt, as far as the mountains of Moab. Sara sat like a queen upon a litter borne by the most prominent of our people. She was bedecked in the finest embroidered linen, perfumed, adorned with ornaments, her hair braided and garlanded with leaves and desert flowers. Hundreds of our people followed her litter: rabbis, children, friends — all but those assigned guard duty and those in the groom's party.

As we watched the procession approach, the maidens detached themselves from the crowd and came toward us, singing. Though it was not quite dark, they carried torches as they walked. Deborah, in the lead, greeted us and led us toward the bride.

Now Aram left our side and, walking beside the litter, gazed at Sara with a look of complete adoration. Though her face was covered with a bridal veil, it was clear that she returned his gaze. The crowd following the bridal couple moved slowly, swaying to the music, singing and dancing, shouting and clapping hands. Some played harps or flutes, or beat timbrels. And I heard the sweet twang of zithers, an ancient and beautiful sound.

Sweet odors of wine and aromatic oil filled the air.

Nuts, parched corn, and other sweetmeats were scattered in the bride and groom's path. High dignitaries, holding myrtle branches in their hands, danced and sang in honor of Sara: "No paint, no powder, and yet a graceful gazelle."

We paraded in this fashion for the length of the plateau, then retraced our steps until we reached the huppah. There, John and I stood as witnesses for a ceremony that should take place a year before the wedding — the kiddushin, or betrothal. But these were not normal times, and there might not be a year for them to share. Eyes fixed on Sara, Aram slipped a gold ring on her finger and said, "Behold, you are consecrated unto me according to the law of Moses and Israel."

Immediately the wedding ceremony followed. Rabbi Hillel recited six benedictions, ending with "Blessed art thou, O Lord, who hast created joy and gladness, bridegroom and bride, mirth and exultation, pleasure and delight, love, brotherhood, peace, and fellowship." I found myself choking with emotion as I thought how brief a life Aram and Sara might have together and how much I longed for such love as they shared.

At last Rabbi Hillel placed his hands on Aram and Sara's heads and, voice trembling, said, "May your days together be long and happy." He cleared his throat several times before adding, "Bless you, my children."

I hugged my brother, then Sara, and whispered, "May you and your children know only peace."

NOW IT WAS TIME to celebrate. Tables had been set with pomegranate juice and jugs of wine, with dates and figs and honey-soaked cakes, with goat cheese and nuts, as in ordinary times. Friends and family crowded around Aram and Sara to wish them well. Dancers, accompanied by flutists and timbrel players, swirled before the couple.

Storytellers stood at their side and told romantic tales of our people.

I remember particularly one such story. An elder, seating himself cross-legged before the bridal couple, proclaimed, "Marriage is made in heaven before birth. It is so!" He nodded his head emphatically, as though some might disagree.

"Forty days before the creation of a child, it is proclaimed in heaven: 'This man's daughter shall marry that man's son.'"

Aram winked at me and smiled happily. I thought of Deborah and wondered if God had promised her to John before birth. And who had been promised to me? Could it be Salome?

"I will tell you a story," the elder continued. We all drew close to listen, because the noise of laughter and singing made it difficult to hear. With wine cups in hand and the flickering of oil lamps lighting our faces, we sat on the ground nearby.

"King Solomon had a daughter. She was the fairest in the land, and he loved her dearly. The king once scanned the stars to discover whom his daughter was destined to marry. When he saw that her future husband would be the poorest man in Judea, he built a high tower by the sea, surrounded it with walls, and placed his daughter in the tower with aged men to guard her. Then Solomon said, 'I shall watch the work of God!'

"In the course of time, a man came upon the tower. Ragged, exhausted from the cold, and nearly starved, he found the carcass of an ox. To escape the fury of the wind, he crawled inside and fell asleep. A bird swooped down, snatched the carcass in which the young man slept, and flew to the tower to consume its remains. There the princess found the young man, awakened him, and ordered food and clothing brought. She fell in love, for he was the handsomest youth in Judea, intelligent and learned as well. Secretly they married.

"When the king learned of the marriage, he rushed to his daughter. 'Who is this young man?' he demanded.

" 'I am but a poor Jew from Acco,' the girl's husband replied, 'but I love your daughter with all my heart.' Then King Solomon knew that there was nothing he could have done to prevent this marriage, for as everyone knows, it is the Lord who chooses a wife for every man."

Many of those listening nodded, believing in his words. But I could not. If it were so, God intended Deborah to be John's wife, not mine.

The old man, encouraged by our attention, went on to tell other stories until Aram and Sara grew weary, and the seated audience began to drift away.

WHEN IT CAME my turn to stand guard duty on the wall, I left unobtrusively. The man I replaced reported that all seemed quiet below. The Roman campfires glowed on the desert floor like lights of a town. From my vantage point, the immediate slopes looked clear.

A balmy night. As I stood my watch, I looked into the distance. Over the immense stretches of sand. Over the desert, silent and eternal. And in the stillness I sensed the strength — the eternal — in our people. For centuries we have lived by God's laws, no matter where we lived or who ruled over us. It is probable that after we are gone, those who follow will also live by the rules that we observe, for it is written in our book of laws what the proper conduct of life should be. There is a bridge, then, between the centuries. I hold hands with the past through these laws that I observe; and the future will reach back to hold my hand.

When John relieved me, I returned to the festivities; the night had grown old. An indolent breeze caused the oil lamps to sputter in the courtyard. Beyond, in the open area, many still celebrated with laughter and songs. A few revelers slept against the walls; others still hummed softly or swayed to the music. But here, where the more intimate friends and close family gathered, the atmosphere had subtly changed. Musicians entertained Sara and Aram, for soon it would be time for them to retire to the bridal chamber.

Their songs were soft and sensual, songs of Solomon:

Behold, thou art fair, my love;
Behold, thou art fair.
Thou hast dove's eyes.

I looked for Deborah and saw her standing alone, listening intently to the singers. It was as if my heart commanded her to notice me, for as I watched her sad, beautiful face, she turned to meet my gaze.

While a flute played soft accompaniment, a male voice passionately intoned,

How fair is thy love, my sister, my spouse!
How much better is thy love than wine!
And the smell of thine ointments than all spices!
Thy lips, O my spouse, drop as the honeycomb:
Honey and milk are under thy tongue;
And the smell of thy garments is like the smell of Lebanon.
A garden enclosed is my sister, my spouse;
A spring shut up, a fountain sealed. . . .
A fountain of gardens, a well of living waters, and streams
*   from Lebanon.*

Awake, O north wind: and come, thou south!
Blow upon my garden, that the spices thereof may flow out.

Suddenly the sweet voice of a woman answered:

Let my beloved come into his garden, and eat his pleasant
fruits.

Deborah lowered her eyes. "Thou art fair, my Deborah, my love," I thought. "Thou hast dove's eyes. But you will never be mine." Deborah turned away and would not look at me again.

The musicians sang on. The night air grew chill, and finally Aram touched Sara's arm and rose. Reaching for her hands, he brought his wife to her feet, his eyes never leaving her face. Then, firmly yet tenderly, he led Sara from the courtyard into the bridal chamber.

Chapter XIII

By Erev Shabbat I had had enough of laughter, wine, and song. I had lost all patience for frivolity. The specter of our plight hung over me like a shroud, and when others tried to drag me into a dance, I smiled and quickly withdrew. There was a gnawing inside me to get on with life. The wedding seemed a postponement, an escape, a setting aside of reality.

My mind returned to the plans for tonight, made a week ago. We had agreed to send a large group to draw water from the hillside cisterns. This would be followed by a raid on the Roman camps on the west. Why was it that something now seemed wrong about the strategy? Reviewing its purpose, its advantages and disadvantages, I felt a foreboding that we had not taken all into consideration.

First, there was my father's reasoning. Everyone knew that to keep our cisterns full, we must make many trips on many nights. Then what kind of arithmetic would send 150 people in one evening to bring up water for one thousand? Considering how much water might be carried, and how many trips could be made while it was still dark, at best those people could supply us with water for perhaps four days. So why the plan for this one evening? And why on the eve of the Sabbath?

And then there was John. His eagerness to stage a raid puzzled me. With thirty or forty men, what could he achieve? Kill a few Romans? What was my peace-loving farmer friend after? Glory! The repugnant word came back again and again because no other answer made sense.

The more I considered this, the more set I became against the raid, and even against my father's orders to obtain water. In the early evening, I finally approached him.

Eleazar was seated at a table beside his bed, a flickering oil lamp for light. Intent on studying the maps spread before him, he did not hear me when I entered.

"Father, I wish to speak with you about tonight's plans," I began.

He looked up and quickly pushed the maps aside. "Yes?" he asked.

"I do not understand what will be gained. Why are you doing this?"

"I have reasons."

"Can you not tell me?" I prodded, wondering why he had been studying maps of the surrounding areas at this time, when the prospects of leaving Masada seemed as remote as rain. "I feel sick at heart. At first I was as excited as the others about the raid, but the more I consider it, the more pointless it seems. John is like a child playing at war!"

My father had risen from the table to place the map rolls in a wall niche. He turned angrily and said, "For weeks now you have been sniping at John. Is it because of Deborah? Do not belittle your friend, Simon. He is the kind of man we need: forceful, courageous, a natural leader. This is no time to carefully weigh alternatives in each hand. It is a time to use those hands!"

"Just for the sake of keeping busy?" I asked sarcastically.

My father's look accused me of disrespect, and I felt momentarily contrite. We stared at each other for a time, neither willing to relent.

"I ask you again, Father. Why tonight? Especially on the eve of the Sabbath?"

"Simon!" he cried in exasperation. "I am testing the Romans' strength and alertness on the west. I want them to think this is where we are most likely to strike.

"If they feel we might attack at the same place again, and that we could well choose the Sabbath again, they might concentrate more strength on the west, drawing attention away from other escape routes."

Silence filled the room. In that space I thought, 'Simon, what a fool!' beginning to see a much larger plan. My father's cheek began to twitch, and as I started to ask another question, he interrupted. "I will not say more, Simon. And do not mention this to anyone. Do I have your word?"

I nodded.

I ENDURED THE SABBATH EVE services only half-involved, reading the prayers automatically, while my mind roamed over my father's words.

"Bâruch atah adenoy . . ." (Did he plan to evacuate most of our people? The women and children?)

"elohenu melech . . ." (Did he plan to attack the Romans' weakest point?)

At dinner I sat engrossed in my thoughts while my mother lit the Sabbath candles and welcomed the day of rest. Sara, blushing self-consciously, served the main dish, a thick soup of nourishing grains, followed by dried figs. My father's silence went unnoticed. Aram carried the conversation, his loquaciousness out of character, yet understandable. He was afraid. Only fifteen, he had never fought before. Disguising his fear with boastful words, he quoted John's pronouncements with unquestioning worship and spilled out gory plans with such ease that I was revolted.

"We will slaughter them," he repeated again and again. "That is what John says. And it is time!"

"Oh, Aram. Do not talk like that!" Sara begged. "It is not like you to be so thirsty for blood."

"John's influence," I remarked bitterly.

"I think for myself," Aram shot back. "You are sick with envy. You wish it had been you who thought of the raid!"

I felt my face flush and almost spit out a like insult, but my father's warning look silenced me.

"Have it your way," I said sullenly, wishing the evening was past.

Envious, Aram had said. Perhaps. My father considered John a natural leader. Aram quoted him incessantly, admired him to the point of worship. People spoke with pride of his fearlessness, his bold imagination. Deborah said she loved him. Could I be so wrong? Was I the only one who saw John as a simple, unimaginative farmer whose main quality was tenacity, whose actions now seemed motivated by less than noble purpose? Had envy so clouded my judgment that I misread John's character and even Deborah's feelings for me?

LATER, AS ARAM AND I blackened our faces with chips of burned wood to be one with the night, my brother apologized.

"Forgive me, Simon. I should not have attacked you like that. But you really have been against John lately. I think I know why."

"I do not want to speak of it," I said.

He smiled. "You know, Salome is a pretty girl. Have you noticed? I think she likes you."

"You better get behind your left ear," I said, ignoring his remark. "That fair skin of yours glows in the dark."

He smeared black dust behind his ear, giving me a conspirator's grin. "Salome is a little plump, perhaps, but all the better. Why not ask Father to speak with Ananus ben Ezra for you?"

"Mind your own affairs!" I exploded. "When I need help in finding a wife, I will ask for it!"

"And I will be here," Aram said, smiling again.

I swallowed hard. To hide my own fears, I over-reacted, a familiar response for me.

"Ready?" I asked Aram. "John said we were to meet as soon as it grew dark." My hand felt constantly for the sword that hung from my belt, as though searching for reassurance. The rocklike knot in my stomach reminded me that my body knew much more than my mind acknowledged. I could not look ahead. It was best to take each moment as it came, and now I just wanted to get on with it so that it could be over.

Suddenly Aram's confidence seemed to drain away. He looked as though he might be sick. "I will be along in a while," he said, his back to me. "You go on." I thought to reassure him, but Aram was a man now, and every man must come to terms with fear in his own way.

Our people had been warned not to interrupt the sounds of wedding celebration while the men were away during the night. How difficult that must have been for them! Those who would walk through the water gates numbered nearly three hundred, twice that originally planned, and represented nearly every family on Masada. Knowing their goal and its dangers, their families nevertheless must keep up the revelry to cover any sounds their men might make. And they did. With faces taut with anxiety, they danced and sang with extra fervor, making enough noise to safeguard the men who were gone. To the Romans below, we Jews must have seemed a curious lot, for it was already the beginning of the third day after the wedding, and though we were under heavy siege, the ecstasy of our celebrants seemed to show no sign of waning.

Guards on our wall had been ordered to douse their torches in the vicinity of the gates, lest the light show those moving out on the paths. I prayed the Romans would not notice this small irregularity, for elsewhere around the wall, where each sentry moved along his route, one could see the glow of torches barely illuminating the sky.

Aram joined us at the last moment, and we moved out quickly. In the lead, walking single file, were those of us who would later attack the Roman camps. Following were the water carriers, all armed. Each man carried four goatskins hanging from a leather harness devised by the tanner. Two skins would hang in front and two in back, heavy loads when full of water, but an efficient means of carrying.

The quarter moon shed little light. We dared not burn torches, but picked our way cautiously, silently, along the familiar paths that led to the water cisterns. Periodically John stopped and raised a hand. Then we all halted and, almost without taking breath, listened. The boisterous revelry of our people came to us clearly, and we were grateful. Below us the Roman camps lay barely visible, small and far away. From them we could hear occasional laughter or song. Sentries made their rounds along the nearly finished wall and called out indistinguishable words from time to time.

To prevent Roman takeover or contamination of our water, we made certain that each of the cisterns was well guarded. Surprisingly, the Romans had made no effort to capture them, though they knew how vital they were to us. I could only suppose they realized such an attempt would be quickly thwarted with a hailstorm of rocks and a shower of arrows.

Our sentries greeted us with welcome embraces. Then we all set to bringing up water as quickly as possible. The level in the wells had dropped to about half full, because there had been no rain in eight months. One rain, and they would be full again. But now, to reach the water, the men had to walk down many steps cut into the caverns, steps unprotected by guard ropes. The way was narrow, and only one man at a time could stand on each step. Since the cisterns were spaced along the eastern and western slopes, only twenty to twenty-five men went to each cavern, and by the time the men in the nearest cistern to the top were ready to return, the men in the second-nearest cistern were nearly ready.

Each man developed a rhythm, so the work progressed well. First came the sound of water gurgling into the narrow neck of the goatskin he was filling, then the splash of a second skin, already full, being drawn out and tied; the heave upward of the heavy containers; the lacing onto the leather harness; and the moving off of two men as soon as they completed their task. Like a human water wheel, carriers with full loads moved up along the cistern paths, while new carriers came down.

The tension eased with each successful trip, and

toward the last, silence was broken by occasional jibes. Standing on the bottom step, hands bracing his aching back while a waterskin filled on the step below, a man might look up and whisper, "This is my woman's work! What am I doing here?" or "Anyone bring a fishing line? Maybe we will be lucky!" His words would echo, and others would joke back till someone above whispered for quiet.

Finally, the last men reached the top, and the cisterns were returned to the sentries.

Now it was time for the raid. Forty of us gathered with John. I glanced at the position of the moon and guessed we still had ample time before first light. The path down was not used as often as the snake path, but it led to a tower which Herod had built to guard the western approach. We had abandoned the tower, for it would have been impossible to hold against the Romans. We suspected they now used it as a lookout.

Working our way down the treacherous slope, we moved more cautiously than before, crouching low whenever we heard a suspicious sound or saw the torch of a Roman sentry. When we were close to the tower, John signaled the group to split up, half on each side of the tower. There they would wait until John, Aram, and I had silenced the guards.

We crept quietly toward the door. Every so often we could see light filling the slits above and supposed it to be a passing guard. I could reconstruct his movement, having stood guard duty in that tower myself many times. He would peer through the slit, then move on to the next along the wall. We could see the light he carried as he passed each window. Thus we could judge when to move and when to stay, and we timed our movements accordingly. Occasionally one of us dislodged a stone, but the noise of our people celebrating above was so fervent that our small sounds went unnoticed.

We felt our way up the narrow stone steps to the room at the top. We could hear the sound of pebbles dropping on the floor, followed by exclamations. Several voices, perhaps. By the regularity of the clicking sound on the wood floor, I judged the soldiers were rolling dice.

I had guessed right. The door above was partially ajar. From the darkness of the landing we could see three men kneeling on the floor. The room was poorly lit, with one oil lamp set in the middle of the floor. A fourth man, the one we had vaguely seen through the tower slits, conscientiously pursued his duty, his back to the others. John pointed to him, then to himself. Aram and I were to take the others. At the last instant I wondered why John had asked Aram to take part in this dangerous assignment. Why had I not protested? But there was no time for doubts.

I moved in quickly, now that the moment to act had come. My heart beat so loudly, I thought it could surely be heard. I felt Aram beside me, but as I thrust my sword into the nearest soldier, Aram seemed to freeze. In the flickering lamplight, I saw him snap the soldier's head back with his arm, but hold his sword aloft. The third man, recovered from his initial surprise, drew his sword and advanced on Aram. Stepping in his way, I drove my sword into his stomach, recognizing a familiar absence of emotion and reason as I did so. Almost immediately I heard movement behind me and leaped aside. I had not found time to withdraw my weapon from the dead man, and reached now for my knife. But it was unnecessary. John had dispatched the sentry and come to Aram's rescue. Shoving him roughly aside, he grabbed the Roman soldier by the hair, yanked back his head, and forced his sword against his throat. The soldier's eyes bulged with terror. John studied him coldly, then, in a voice I had never heard before, commanded, "Aram, come here!"

Aram rose from where he had fallen. A peculiar smile distorted his lips. Even in the poor light I could see it. I wanted to shake him, strike him to make him stop grinning, but something in John's voice kept me from intruding.

"Do it!" John commanded. "Now!"

Aram shook his head. Tears rolled down his face, though the strange smile still quivered on his lips.

Never taking his eyes from the prisoner's face, John repeated, "Do it! I command you." But Aram remained frozen, grinning and sobbing soundlessly.

Still holding the prisoner's head so the terrified eyes stared at him, John bent and thrust his knee into the man's back. With his other hand now free, he forced the sword handle into Aram's unwilling hand. Then, guiding his rigid arm, John raised it aloft, and with one sure, sudden stroke, brought the blade down upon the prisoner's neck.

It happened so quickly, I gasped. Blood spurted everywhere. My hands and tunic were covered with it. John stood in a puddle of it. Aram, legs wet with blood, stared in horror at the decapitated Roman and dropped the sword as though it seared his hand. He shivered and cried, "No, no!"

"Stop that!" John whispered furiously. "Get out of the way!"

I grabbed Aram's shoulder and spun him toward the stairway, leading him as though he were blind. He moaned, a haunting sound, as though he cried for all the ills of man through all the centuries of time.

I sensed emotion returning in me — compassion for Aram and loathing for John — and shook my head, as if the physical action would force it back. No time for that now. By remaining human, Aram had challenged the mechanical, unthinking, unfeeling act of killing to survive. Humanity and killing are incompatible. I had learned that long ago. Aram would learn it too, if given another chance.

The fresh air cleared my head of the awful stench of blood. But it did nothing for Aram, who remained dazed, unable to move or think for himself. John emerged from the building behind us and quickly appraised Aram's condition.

"We must leave him," he whispered, glancing at the stars. "Hide him somewhere."

I led Aram to a deeply shadowed side of the building and eased him down. He looked uncomprehendingly at the blood on his legs, trembling. "Aram," I whispered gently, "stay here. We will be back for you — soon." Then I ran to join the others.

The men started to move off as soon as John reappeared. One group made its way toward the smaller and closer of the two Roman camps, built to eventually keep us from the cisterns. The second group, mine, moved stealthily toward the large camp, which we believed to be the headquarters of the Roman commander. It was outside the circumvallation wall, and a greater distance away.

In a little while it would begin to grow light. The south wind blew gently, bringing occasional snatches of music from above. I could hear a sentry on the wall, whistling softly, but little sound came from the Roman camps. John dispatched a man to silence each guard patroling the wall, and after a short wait, we were able to scale it and reach the other side. I thought to myself, "I am outside, and free! I could leave this place and never return!" But it was only a fleeting thought.

At last we reached the main camp. The stillness was so profound I could hear a man, perhaps ten paces away, sigh in his sleep. Standing in the shadow of the camp wall, each of us dipped the wooden stake he had brought into a container of oil and quickly set it ablaze. Then, moving off swiftly so that we were well apart, we hurled our burning brands onto the tents of the sleeping Roman Tenth Legion.

Chapter XIV

I leaped from my cot, fully clothed, even before Marius burst into my tent. He did not need to explain a thing. I could judge by the wild noise of confusion without. Cries of pain, shouted orders, moans mingled with the acrid smell of scorched cloth and flesh.

"How bad?" I demanded, lacing my sandals as I spoke.

"Bad. The wind blows from the southwest. The fire spread swiftly. The entire camp is threatened."

"Accident?"

"Attack. Cestius's camp, too."

Grimly I nodded. That meant they had killed the tower guards, or we would have been warned. It also meant we would find our wall sentries dead.

"Come!" I said.

Outside, black smoke and cinders filled the air. A searing wind, crackling sharply, searched in gusts. Nearby, a tent flapped and bent against the wind like some animal in pain. Then, suddenly, it burst into flames. Men rushed forward with buckets of water. Others ran away from the blaze, leading badly burned friends. I saw one man, skin smoldering, grope blindly for escape. It was bad. Very bad.

I could not guess how much time had elapsed since the enemy struck. Had they fired burning arrows at our camp from the circumvallation wall? If so, they were probably already safely up the hill.

The circumvallation wall! Built to imprison the Jews! As I galloped out the gate leading a large force of cavalry, I realized that wall would just as well impede our pursuit. Our horses could not jump its height. There was no breach close enough through which we might ride — except through Cestius's camp. Flames exploding skyward spoke for the confusion there.

Frustrated by my inability to pursue the enemy except on foot, I ordered our men to dismount and scale the wall.

It was not yet dawn, and the smoke from Cestius's camp hung over the landscape, making visibility even more difficult. I peered through the haze from the top of the wall, cursing my old eyes for not seeing what must be there. Ordering my men to direct their arrows at the path above the tower, whether or not they could see the Jewish raiders, I led a patrol over the wall and started up the slope.

Beyond the fires, the air cleared somewhat, but visibility remained poor. The sun had risen; I could see a faint glow toward the top of the rock. But this was the western slope, still in deep shadow. At the tower, I found our men dead, as expected. I could barely make out movement on the hillside just below the cisterns. The Jews had too great a lead; still, I was determined to pursue them.

Avoiding the winding path, we scrambled upward, a torturous job, for the slope was dry, and rocks slid away underfoot. We had made considerable progress nevertheless, when suddenly I felt the earth tremble under my hands. I threw myself flat against the ground, knowing instantly what it must be. Rocks came hurtling by, bouncing and crashing downward in a deafening roar. I hugged the ground, feeling the tremor in every bone, while the men nearby mumbled prayers. And the gods must have heard. As the last rocks tumbled to the ground below, I realized that, by some miracle, not one of us was hurt.

Whether it was the gods, or luck, or the Jews' poor aim, I could not say. But this I note: directly above us a ledge protruded in such a way that rocks which struck there arced outward, then fell harmlessly far below.

By the time we could move on, the Jews had reached the protection of their cisterns. It was pointless to pursue them now. Archers on the wall might do them harm, but the distance worked against us.

MUCH LATER, in my tent, I interviewed Marius and my cohort commanders individually to learn how our security could have been so lax. It quickly became clear where fault lay. Marius had been in charge of the western defense. He assigned guard duty.

When I challenged him, he became agressive, evasive. "I do not know how this happened," he said. "We had four men in the tower, and the wall was adequately patrolled."

"Then how could a handful of men do so much damage? Where were those guards — asleep?"

Marius's face went white as parchment. His eyes were red from sleeplessness, the skin below puffed, though not, I suspected, from attention to duty. He had undoubtedly been up with his camp harlots until shortly before the attack.

Studying the tabletop as though it presented some

interesting problem, he shook his head slowly. "I planned security well, I tell you. There were enough guards. I am sure of it."

"Then why were we surprised?" I questioned icily.

Again he shook his head. "I do not deserve all the blame," he protested. "We have been here nearly two months, and never have the Jews attempted anything so bold. Who would think they would dare?"

"Obviously not you."

"No, I did not. But, Flavius, who would have thought — during the celebration? On their Sabbath?"

He had suddenly hit upon a line of reasoning that looked promising, and his face grew sly. "Even you said the Jews were probably celebrating some high holiday. When you questioned that prisoner, Ananias, he said it was a wedding, and that they would be occupied with it for a week. Remember?"

"Fool! And you believed him?"

"Of course. You did not?"

"About the celebration, yes. But that they would be occupied with revelry — solely — for a week, no. And I told you this."

"You did not! I am sure," Marius replied.

Almost immediately I recognized his game. Rather than defend himself against my accusation or admit his error, he would counterattack. I felt impatient with this game, for we had played it often enough. He was not a worthy opponent. He would lose to me now as he had always lost, for the same reason: he never thought far enough ahead.

Usually I silenced him before he made an absolute fool of himself. This time, however, though my patience was all but gone, I decided I would not interrupt. Let him weave his own trap word by word until he enmeshed himself in the threads of illogic like a fly in a spider's web.

My silence must have encouraged him, for his face became animated. "I saw no need to double the guard! The celebration was only in its third night, their Sabbath eve at that. Everyone knows these Jews do not work on the Sabbath, much less fight. Especially fight! Even you have said it is laziness on their part!" He looked triumphant, thinking he had bested me at last.

I had listened long enough. "Marius. You were at Jotapata, were you not?" I asked.

He looked at me suspiciously before nodding.

"Through the entire siege, I believe. As I recall, you were commended for exceptional bravery. Is that not so?"

He flushed and stood straighter. "Yes, Flavius," he said without hesitation.

"What were Vespasian's orders for the Sabbath?"

"He gave many orders!"

"Indeed. Let me be more explicit. Each day of the week your forces executed the siege at a systematic pace. But on the Sabbath, was this pace abated or intensified?"

He seemed to collapse as he recognized where I had led him. "On the Sabbath, Vespasian ordered us to double our efforts against the enemy," he mumbled.

"What? I did not hear you!"

"We doubled our efforts against the enemy."

"Yes, and what did the Jews do on the Sabbath days when we Romans doubled our efforts? Did they rest?"

"No — Flavius," he admitted. "Josephus, their general, would not let them. Instead, they fought back as hard as they knew how."

I recognized a brief hesitation preceding his answer. Marius had almost lapsed into familiarity, for the months of close association and the experience in the prisoners' camps had bound us together as reluctant mates. But there was not a trace of friendliness in me now as I placed the blame directly on him.

"They fought back as hard as they knew how at Jotapata, on their day of rest. Knowing that, why in the name of Jupiter did you not have the foresight to double the guard here? Do you know what losses we have suffered because of you?"

He nodded and lowered his eyes.

"How many men lost in Cestius's camp?"

"Thirty-five," he murmured uncomfortably. "Fifty more badly burned."

"And that is only the count in Cestius's camp. What were the losses here?"

He held up his hands in a gesture of surrender and gave me a conciliatory smile, but his eyes filled with hatred. "I admit I made a serious mistake in judging the Jews. Exile me to the deserts of Idumea, if you wish." He laughed uneasily. "But Flavius, hear me out. I will make it up. Believe me."

Could I trust Marius's judgment again? When I first considered him for my second in command, I not only found his record impressive but responded to his spirited personality.

By nature I am a dull man, a man of few surprises, and army life, except for the brief days spent in battle, drags along tediously year after year. I foresaw the long days and months of military routine relieved by Marius's enthusiasm and wit, enlivened by his intellectual challenge. As commander, I must limit my friendships to those close to me in rank; to find a second in command who would not only be effective but might provide stimulating companionship was indeed a great boon!

How wrong — to have mistaken cunning for cleverness, and equated brashness with sharpness of mind. Marius's intelligence had the depths of a birdbath; his wit, the murkiness of a stagnant pool. And he drank too much and had a mercurial temper. If anything should befall me, what would become of the legion?

On the other hand, he worked hard, and the men would do anything for him. While they respected me, Marius they loved. His brashness and earthy humor were the very things the men liked most about him. To replace him now would be greeted with resentment in the ranks. It would slow our siege operations. I had no real choice. Despite his error in judgment, Marius must remain until we took Masada.

"The damage is done," I said wearily. "Laying blame does not bring back the dead or erase this shame, that our defenses could so easily be penetrated! We must get that ramp built! Until it is done, we cannot bring up the battering ram to break through to the Jews. We cannot do them serious damage!"

"I will drive the prisoners harder so that it will soon be finished," Marius said, trying to make amends. "I will double the work force and start the engineers on the siege machine. I will —"

"No, Marius," I interrupted. "Cestius will take over as defense chief of this sector, and I myself will oversee the ramp construction. You will assume command of the eastern defenses — and do better, I expect, than you did here." Though I could not remove Marius altogether from his command, I could place him in a less sensitive position.

"The ramp project was to be mine!" he argued. "We discussed it months ago. Flavius, do not send me away from the real challenge! I may as well be exiled to Idumea. Guarding the eastern sector is child's play!"

I knew how much Marius wanted and needed the dramatic opportunity that the ramp offered. Such a position would place him shoulder to shoulder with large numbers of soliders and prisoners. His flamboyant style thrived in such a situation, evoking admiration and applause. Though I felt almost sorry for him, I could no longer abide his presence in my camp. "Those are my orders," I said. "You will assume command of the easterm camps immediately."

Marius's face lost its arrogance and took on a look of self-doubt. Realizing I defeated myself by making this assignment seem a punishment, I tried to breathe purpose into it. Without a sense of worth, Marius would be useless to me.

"The work goes too slowly there," I relented. "It may be that the Jews will attack on the east now, believing we have been convinced that only the west is vulnerable." I did not really think this to be so, but my words offered Marius some hope.

"True," he said thoughtfully. "This attack may have been a foil to divert our attention." He considered the idea for a moment longer then solemnly declared, "I now assume that command, as you order, Flavius. And this I swear. A surprise attack will not be possible. Nor shall any escape down the snake path — not while I am in control." His eyes glittered with determination.

I knew Marius would not fail a second time. Should a problem develop on the east, he would be well prepared.

Chapter XV

Since I last wrote in this journal, they started a new kind of building. It began soon after the raid and continues ceaselessly, day after day.

Enormous boulders, large quantities of dirt, and all manner of rocks are being brought to the western side. Jewish prisoners are laying these materials on the neck of land that slopes from our wall to the desert. They are broadening the ridge, and it is easy to see their intent. They will raise the slope to bring their machines within reach of our walls, the very thing I feared the Romans might do and promised Deborah they never could. But that was long ago. Almost three months ago. A lifetime. Before the legion came. When we were young and full of dreams, when promises could be made and kept.

We have not been idle. Every day since they started this new work, we have rolled rocks down on the laborers or harried them with arrows. But the Romans have met this kind of resistance before, and they have provided the workers with leather shields, which they carry over themselves as they crawl up the slope, lugging materials. They resemble huge brown turtles creeping along. Our weapons strike and bounce off these shields, rarely causing harm.

Since our night attack, the Romans seem more determined. They keep up a steady barrage of arrows when we attempt to deter the works. Rather than risk certain death, our men must seek the protection of the towers at such times.

Since the raid, Aram has been ill. His fever subsided quickly, but he remains morose. Though my father is greatly disturbed by his condition, I do not think he suspects John's part in it, and I will not enlighten him.

He is so proud of John. At a recent ceremony in which he praised all who participated in the attack, he elevated him to the rank of second in command. It was a mockery to hear my father call him a man "who places his men's needs and safety before his own, a man who is a friend to his sons, and a son in his home." I do not quarrel with John's military talent now, but I can no longer consider him a friend.

Close friends think that marriage has tamed Aram's playful nature. My mother worries that Sara and he are unhappy, and she tries to give them greater privacy.

It is Sara who comes closest to the truth. She sought me out at Ananus ben Ezra's office one afternoon, waiting until all the patients had gone so that she might speak with me alone.

"What is wrong with Aram?" she asked directly, lowering her voice so the doctor might not hear. I knew at once her meaning.

"Who is with you, Simon?" Ananus ben Ezra called from the next room, where he had been lying down. He has been ill of late, coughing and wheezing until he becomes exhausted. He blames his condition on the dust and dryness.

When I told him it was Sara, he came into the room to greet her, and though he himself looked haggard, he asked after Aram.

"That is why I am here," Sara said, allowing the doctor to take her hand. "Since the raid, Aram has been a different person. And it is not the illness, I think. It has something to do with what happened on the raid."

Ananus ben Ezra nodded. "I have noticed it, too," he said. "The fever has passed. But some other thing lingers."

"Have you spoken to Aram about it, Sara?" I asked.

"Oh, yes," she replied. "Many times. I have said, 'Aram, what makes you so unhappy? Did something happen the night of the raid, for since you returned, you are so changed. Or is it something I have said or done?'"

"And what does Aram answer?"

"He says, 'What could have happened that did not happen to everyone else? Who have you been talking to? Has anyone said I did not behave as a man?' — What kind of words are these? I did not suggest he lacks courage. What is *wrong* with him?"

"It is difficult for a man to kill for the first time," I replied.

"I know that!" she answered impatiently. "But there must be more than that. Before the raid, every other word he spoke was 'John.' Now Aram never mentions his name, and John has not once come to see Aram since then. What happened between them?"

"I cannot tell you anything," I said.

"But you *must*, Simon," she said, beginning to cry. "If I do not know what troubles Aram, I cannot help him. It is ruining everything between us. It is as if he festers in here!" She touched her heart.

I lowered my eyes, for suddenly the vision of John forcing Aram's sword-clenched hand took shape before me, and I feared my face reflected the horror I felt.

Sara did not seem to notice. She talked on, exploring every possibility that had occurred to her. "If he is unhappy because of me, I could go back to my parents' home . . ."

"No, Sara, it is not that," I protested, wishing she would end this conversation. "He will be all right. Just be patient."

"I cannot! What does he see when he wakes at night, stares at the ceiling, and shivers? It is something unbearable."

Poor Sara. She had come so close to the truth that I wanted to tell her the whole of it, but could not. It was for Aram to tell.

THE RAID has had its effect on all of us. On Aram, who must feel less a man. On Sara, who now feels left out of his life. On me, for I bear a grudge against John that grows deeper each day. On John, whose new confidence borders on arrogance. And even on Deborah, who appears wary and distrustful in John's company.

John is so preoccupied, I do not think he has noticed Deborah's unease. His attention is taken — by the troops who demand his time, by the worshipful children who follow him everywhere, and even by the young women who smile at him with hopeful eyes.

I try to fill the days with activity so I have no time to think of Deborah. Yet she is always there, only waiting for a quiet moment to appear. Is it because she and John have failed to set a wedding date? Do I find hope in that?

It requires the greatest effort of will to keep myself from seeking her out. Sometimes, when I am tending a patient, some instinct suddenly interrupts my thoughts, and I know that if I went to a particular place on our plateau, she would be there. The presentiment is so strong that though my body stays behind because my mind commands it to, my senses struggle against reason and escape to her.

One day, to test if it were but imagination urging me on, I left my work and went to the place my feet carried me. With heart pounding, I walked quickly, hoping she would not be there, so there would be an end to these daydreams. But she was.

As soon as I came out upon the lowest tier of Herod's palace, I saw her. Children played with pebbles and a ball near her feet, yet she seemed oblivious to them. She leaned upon the wall, back to me, and the wind whipped her hair forward, hiding her face. Even when I was only a few paces away and children had shouted my name in greeting, she did not seem to hear. When I touched her shoulder, she turned and looked at me without recognition. Tears stood in her eyes.

"What is wrong, Deborah?" I asked.

She shook her head.

A young boy pulled at her gown. She bent and picked him up. The child wound his arms around her neck and kissed her, then struggled to be released.

Instead of speaking to me directly, she turned again to the view of the Sea of Salt and the mountains of Moab.

"It is John," she said. "I do not understand him anymore. He has changed."

"We have all changed," I answered evasively.

"Oh, Simon!" she cried impatiently. "You sound like Rabbi Hillel, always smoothing over fears with words that mean nothing. You know what I mean. We have not *all* changed. Not as John has."

I could not bring myself to judge John. If Deborah would ever love me, I did not want her affection to grow from my destruction of his character.

"He told me what happened in the tower," she said, with a bitterness unlike her.

"About Aram?" I asked, stunned.

"Yes — what Aram could not do. I cannot believe John could be so cruel."

She turned to face me. "Why did he tell me? Was he proud of it? When I told him he was as heartless as the Romans, he laughed!"

She began to cry again. I wanted to hold and comfort her. Instead, I found myself defending John. "We are under siege, Deborah. It was kill or be killed."

"Then why could John not do the deed himself? Tell me that!"

I shrugged. "Perhaps he believed that he had to harden Aram, that if Aram could kill once, the next time would not be so difficult."

Deborah covered her face with her hands and shook her head. With muffled voice she said, "I believed in John — in his goodness! Who can I believe in now?"

"Deborah, listen," I urged. "John was in command. He acted as he thought best, and maybe it was best. At a time like that, one cannot be soft or hesitant."

"If we all become savage brutes, then what will it matter who wins?" she asked, looking at me through tear-filled eyes.

"I think you are placing too much importance on this."

"Do you think so?" she asked. "That is what John said. But then I told him about my grandfather." She shook her head in disbelief. "Grandfather has taken to wandering at night. One night one of our guards mistook

120

him for a Roman and nearly killed him. Do you know what John said?"

I did not answer.

"That perhaps it would have been better if the guard *had* killed him. The old are a drain on our food and water supplies and of no use against the enemy. Do you understand now?"

I found no words to respond to Deborah's fears. She was right. John had changed. We all had changed. Stress erodes character. Already we had all displayed, to varying degrees, fear, cowardice, greed, arrogance, even tyranny. How much more of decency would be compromised in this fight? If we had chosen peace, we would have had to sacrifice freedom. Yet, by choosing freedom, must we sacrifice compassion, honor, love — all that makes us human?

Chapter XVI

I had not seen much of John since the raid. It came as a surprise, therefore, when he entered Ananus ben Ezra's office one evening and asked to speak with me. I was boiling water on the cooking stone, trying to bring moisture to the dry room, testing the doctor's theory that the dryness caused his exhausting coughing spells.

"Your father wishes to see you, Simon. You are to come with me," John said with a new aloofness.

As I bent over the doctor to hear if his breathing came easier, I wondered why John had been sent for me when any foot soldier could have carried this message. Ananus ben Ezra's face had taken on some color, but I had not realized before how fragile he had become.

"I will be all right," the physician whispered with obvious effort. "Do not worry. Go along."

John and I found nothing to say to each other as we crossed the plateau and entered the synagogue together. My father and Rabbi Hillel were in the room behind the sanctuary, seated at a table, in an expectant silence. Between them lay a roll of maps, the same ones my father had been studying some weeks ago.

As soon as we were seated, my father leaned toward us. "We have decided to arrange someone's escape. John says we will need your help," he said.

I glanced at John, but he was studying the floor.

"You know of Joseph ben Matthias," my father continued. "The Romans now call him Flavius Josephus."

Of course. Everyone knew Josephus, our most brilliant and important general in the first years of the war. He had recruited and trained a hundred thousand of our men in Roman methods of fighting. It was through his leadership that we achieved our early victories. But many of our people saw him as an opportunist rather than a dedicated leader. And this had proved to be true. When Jotapata fell to Vespasian's legions, Josephus surrendered willingly, while others of our leaders preferred to end their own lives rather than concede. His resourcefulness as a Jewish general was nothing compared to his resourcefulness as a prisoner. By predicting General Vespasian's accession to the throne, he immediately won favor and protection. By providing the Romans with information and advice on our strengths, positions, and methods of fighting, he gained prestige and power. Josephus had done much to hasten our defeat. Many believed that, to further his personal ambitions, he sold Judea to the Romans. Our people despised him.

"What has Josephus to do with us now?" I asked, puzzled.

Rabbi Hillel spoke. "It is believed that he is in Rome, writing a history of our war against the Romans. Do you realize what that means?"

I shook my head.

"He will write an account that makes the Romans

123

appear noble and righteous, and the Jews seem scoundrels and fools. He dares not give history the true picture of our fight, for by doing so he would lose Roman favor. His future depends on their affection. So he must condemn us, while he endows our enemy with the most noble intentions. We must not allow future generations to know only what Josephus will set down."

"But he dare not write what has not really happened," I protested. "Others who served under him — his own troops, too — will know the truth."

"There is some truth to that. Oh, what happened will be no doubt reported accurately." My father spoke with irony. "But *why* it happened will be Josephus's interpretation. That is what we fear."

The idea startled me. But what could we do about it?

"Before it is too late — and it may already be — we must send a spokesman from our fortress to inform those elsewhere why we hold out and what we fight for. And it must be done soon. For if the Romans take Masada," the rabbi said sadly, "they may leave none of us to carry the truth abroad."

In the long silence that followed, my mind traveled beyond Masada, to the wall that encircled us, to the towers which protected that wall, to the Romans in their camps outside that wall. Who could get through to the outside?

When I asked that question, my father replied, "We have thought of this for some time. Rabbi Hillel feels we must not make a general appeal, for it would arouse greater anxiety. And there might be too many who would argue to go. We felt it must be someone close to the leadership. John suggested you."

"*Me?*" The shock of John's suggesting me — *to get rid of me?* — hit hard. "Impossible!" I said. "I will not go.

Leave you all, knowing what you face? No. I could not! Besides, Ananus ben Ezra is very ill. He cannot do without me. Many need medical attention."

My father glanced at the rabbi. "That you do not want to go is inconsequential. You are *needed*."

"But it is true what he says about ben Ezra, Eleazar," the rabbi said, stroking his beard. "I agree. I do not know how much longer he can tolerate those coughing spells. His heart is not strong, you know."

"Why not John?" I asked. "He could go. *He* knows every hill, every spring. He is resourceful. He would stand the best chance of getting away."

"We need him here," my father responded.

"Then who?"

"Aram?" John asked.

"Aram — yes!" I reacted, feeling sudden relief. "Aram and Sara!" At least this offered them a chance.

"Aram is not well," my father said.

"True," I agreed, "but he knows this area as well as any of us. Further, we could manage without him, and he meets all your requirements."

Almost to himself, John added, "Aram *and* Sara. Together they would arouse less attention. But they would have to get out by the snake path. The west is too heavily guarded now."

"Aram could not manage it," my father argued. "He would surely meet resistance getting over the wall, and he is not tough enough to handle it. Sara would be an encumbrance."

I was surprised to realize he recognized Aram's weakness.

"We could help," John said, jumping from his seat to stand beside me. "Simon and I could get them over the wall," he said with certainty.

"Yes," I told my father and the rabbi. "John and I could subdue the men on the wall and lead Aram and Sara safely over." John nodded agreement, and I felt something of our old friendship in that gesture.

"Eleazer?" the rabbi inquired, looking at my father.

"Perhaps. With Simon and John's help, it may work," he said.

And so it was decided that on the first cloudy or rainy night, John and I would escort Sara and Aram down the snake path and over the wall — so that they might tell the truth about why we fight on Masada.

Chapter XVII

The first rain came late in the month of Kislev, after the Festival of Lights. It was long overdue, and yet it arrived unexpectedly. One midday, the sand began to swirl, and it became hard to breathe. Black clouds appeared suddenly from the north and in a short time passed over, delivering a drenching shower.

After so many months of heat and drought, it seemed a miracle. I ran, with everyone else, to stand beneath the sky and to drink in the delicious sweetness. We laughed and sang and thanked God, and cried with happiness, and watched with wonder as water pelted the thirsty land. Soon rain pooled on the ground, and children splashed and wallowed in the mud, delighting in the unfamiliar squoosh their bare feet made as they were sucked into the muck with every step. After the rain, the air smelled fresh and clean. The damp earth showed shoots of green bent over like tiny worms.

The Romans did not fare so well. A portion of the ramp they are constructing slid away, and the sand will be heavy with water now, making construction harder.

Wadi Nimrein overflowed, flushing mud and rocks into their nearest camp. The breach they had made in the aqueducts months ago caused water to rush through and cascade down the mountainside in a powerful and beautiful fall. The desert floor, at least for a few days, would be mud and slime.

We had planned to wait for a cloudy night to cover Aram and Sara's escape through the Roman lines, but now that the circumvallation wall was complete, escape would be as difficult one day as the next. And so we agreed to wait for the optimum conditions: rain would offer more cover than darkness; a moonless night would be best.

We compromised. On a night with a half moon, the wind came up, clouds hid the moon, and the sky looked threatening. Then the wind died, and a steady, misty rain began that blocked visibility beyond a few paces. It was an unusual rain for this part of the country, more like those on the coast, but ideal for an escape.

Even before the rain started, I knew we would be able to go, and so arranged for Ananus ben Ezra's comfort before the messenger arrived. My friend and teacher was extremely ill. In the daytime he sat with other patients in the sun and fresh air, and though his face grew ruddy from exposure, his breathing remained labored, and his pulse fast and irregular. The dry air seemed bad for him, and the moist air no better; he coughed and drew painful breaths and had not the strength to stand. Even on this evening, I could do little. His wife scurried back and forth, plying him with every remedy, till he cried out that she must let him be, or surely he would die of her kindness.

She even argued with me, imploring that I bleed him again or swaddle him in blankets in a closed, heated room. When I showed her how much easier he seemed to breathe with the door open to the air, she finally conceded, but did not truly trust what she saw. Eventually she retired to a corner, looking frightened and forlorn, consciously drawing each breath as though for her husband.

When the messenger came for me, I felt I could not go, yet knew I must. Ananus understood. As I adjusted the bolsters behind his head, he smiled and whispered, "Take care, Simon, and do not worry."

I met John in the courtyard leading to my family's apartment. Together we went in and found a place where we could change into sheepskins to disguise ourselves, blacken our faces, and check our weapons.

Sara, pale as alabaster, shivered as though with chill. Hands clenched tightly against her breast, she listened to her parents' soft-spoken encouragement. Her mother wiped tears away, but not once did she take her eyes from Sara's face. Words spilled from Sara's father without pause, as though he feared she might disappear if he should take even one breath. And Sara stared at them, wide-eyed, unable to stop shivering.

Nearby, Aram checked the contents of the pack he would carry against a list my father read aloud to him. I felt anxious for my brother, but he seemed calm, despite the journey ahead. Earlier he had confided that he hoped to redeem himself by this assignment. And that he trusted John and I could get Sara and him safely past the Romans. When the pack was finally adjusted to Aram's back, the rabbi stepped forward.

"When you reach Damascus, you will remember where to go and with whom to speak?"

"Yes, yes," Aram replied with tolerant impatience, for he had recited the names and places with the rabbi countless times. "And Sara knows them too."

But Rabbi Hillel had to be sure. "If the Jewish community at Damascus no longer exists, what will you do?"

"Move on to Antioch, where we must find Joshua ben Arach, or the Rabbi Gamliel."

"And if neither of these men still lives?"

Aram thought a moment, then answered, "Find any remaining member of the Sanhedrin."

"And failing that?"

"Find the head of the synagogue."

"And failing that?"

"The director of charity . . ." And so Aram continued down the list in a methodical recitation that seemed to please the rabbi.

"Now, what will you tell these men?"

"That they must organize a force to rescue those on Masada," Aram said, shrugging his shoulders to ease the load on his back.

My father gave Rabbi Hillel a knowing look.

"More important," the rabbi said kindly, "is that you make it clear, very clear, that we *do* resist the Romans, and *why*."

Aram nodded. Then suddenly his eyes blurred with tears. Perhaps he realized for the first time what this mission really meant. Until now, he had been convinced he and Sara were being sent primarily to organize a rescue army. My father's reasons for their selection had seemed logical: that Sara could find her way in the cities where they were to go; that he knew how to reach those cities without using the roads; and that a man and a woman traveling together would arouse less suspicion.

But the look that had passed between my father and the rabbi, and the rabbi's insistence on the importance of the message Aram must deliver, gave new meaning to the facts. It was surely too late to organize a resistance from outside. He and Sara were being sent away for only one purpose: to deliver the message that we were not irresponsible cutthroats, as many had heard Josephus claim, but ordinary citizens resisting Roman tyranny and defending our freedom, regardless of the cost.

Aram sought my father's eyes. They verified his new insight. "Father!" he blurted, and his hands reached out to him.

"Do not fear, my son. All will be well. We are in God's hands."

My mother rose and clasped Aram fiercely, then broke away and covered her face. "Be good to Sara. Take care. Take care," she murmured.

The rabbi blessed them. My father opened the door. In a voice that would not abide disagreement, he said, "It is time to go." And Aram, walking as though in a dream, obeyed. Sara did not follow immediately, held by her mother's anguished sobs. My father kindly but firmly drew Sara away.

"She will be all right, Rachel," he said gently. "Now give her your blessings, and let her go." Sara's mother nodded but continued to sob as she released her daughter.

Sara ran back to embrace her mother one last time. Then she turned and hurried after Aram.

THE GUARDS at the snake-path gate and in the towers nearest to it had been told only a short while before that we would be passing through. They looked at us with curiosity and perhaps hostility, but accepted my father's orders without question. Quickly we slipped through the gate and started down the first winding of the snake path.

Wary as deer, we descended in silence, staying close together, one behind the other, for it was difficult to see more than a few paces ahead. Under the best conditions, the snake path is no easy walk. Now it proved treacherous, muddy and obstructed by sand and rocks washed down from the recent downpour. In one place we had to clear the dirt away so we could go on. Thunder rumbled halfheartedly in the mountains across the Sea of Salt, but there were no flashes of light to illuminate the dark.

I did not think back to the moments before we left, or ahead to what we must do on the wall. Rather, I found myself enjoying the rain. The soft sound as the drops struck the dirt and the good smell of it made me feel safe and content. It brought back vivid memories of spring rains in the north. The four of us seemed bound together through need and love, moving as through some misty dream.

But the feeling was short-lived. Too soon we saw the end of the path and the base of the rock.

When we reached the desert floor, a thin sheet of water flowed over the land in the direction we moved, pushing us swiftly forward. We walked four abreast now, with Aram and Sara in the middle. John, slightly in the lead, peered through the darkness in the direction of the Roman wall. Suddenly I sensed a slight breeze and felt a rush of panic as I imagined the wind coming up and driving the clouds away, exposing us. But the sky remained as still and impenetrable as before, and we moved on.

The area nearest the start of the snake path was extremely well fortified. We had noticed that from the top, and so had headed as far north as we could until we judged ourselves to be beyond the large camp, probably past the smaller one as well. Only then did we approach the Roman wall, grateful for the cover of darkness. At its base we crouched and listened, but heard no sound other than the muted whisper of rain. We could barely make out lights in the two nearest towers, and judged we must be halfway between them.

Now we had to wait until we determined the number of sentries patrolling the wall and their positions. In this we were fortunate. Though we kept an ear to the wall in hopes of picking up some sound from the guards as they approached, we did not recognize their coming until they were almost above us. Two sentries stopped midway between the towers and leaned over the wall, studying the nearby terrain and talking of the miserable weather. Sara gasped as she realized their proximity, then clapped her hands over her mouth. It seemed certain they would see us, but they did not.

After a time the men continued in opposite directions. We guessed that each guard would check in at the tower to which he was headed. If we eliminated these guards, they would be quickly missed. Even if we succeeded in killing those in the two towers as well (a highly risky venture), what of the sentries on the other sides of the towers, those who would be reporting in? It seemed best to chance helping Aram and Sara over the wall before the men returned. And given the possibility that other guards were moving away from the nearest towers as these two headed toward them, we had to work very quickly.

John and I scaled the wall, making as little sound as possible. From its top we reached down to help first Sara, then Aram. As soon as Aram joined us, we lowered him to the opposite side of the wall so he could help Sara from below. Then we jumped, joining them — and just in time. Below the wall we all huddled together and waited as the sentries passed again, exchanging routine greetings.

Again I felt a breeze on my face. John must have felt it too, for he frowned and looked quickly at the sky. The drizzle seemed to be lessening; the sky appeared lighter.

On his signal we moved forward again, about ten paces beyond the wall. There we stopped. "We must go back now," John whispered, grasping Aram's and Sara's hands, "and you must hurry, for it may grow light now that the rain is ending."

My brother's voice quivered. "Good-bye, my friend," he said to John warmly.

Then he turned to me. We embraced, conscious that each moment we took meant one moment less of darkness, of safety, yet more conscious that we might never meet again.

"Safe journey," I whispered to them both. Then, not daring to waste another moment, I nudged them gently forward, away from Masada. Good-bye, Aram, my brother, my friend.

JOHN AND I were well beyond the wall and headed back up the snake path when the wind shifted, driving the rain clouds swiftly across the sky, toward the northwest. The moon alternately appeared and disappeared, and the rain stopped.

We climbed rapidly, trying to get as far up the path as possible before the clouds disappeared, exposing the slope to the moon.

We must have been but a third of the way up, and beginning to feel hopeful that Aram and Sara were well on their way, when a sharp, agonized scream pierced the air and almost immediately faded in the wind. John and I stiffened, straining to hear more.

"Sara?" John barely whispered, too horrified to finish the thought. Then, hopefully, "The kill of a jackal?"

I shook my head.

A soft light began to sweep over the slope as the moon

broke through a cloud directly above Masada. At the same instant we heard the cry again, a despairing sob.

I spun around and ran back down the path. John commanded me to stop, but I would not listen; I only knew I had to get to them. "Come back! It is too late!" he shouted, just as arrows began to fly. Only then did I return to my senses. Dropping face down on the ground so as to make as small a target as possible, I lay panting, while arrows whistled above, below, and all around me.

I lay there for what seemed a long time, feeling sick and helpless. By the time the onslaught stopped, the moon had vanished behind the rock of Masada. Darkness at last. I saw the lights of torches moving along the path below, and heard voices raised in sharp commands. Struggling to my feet, I groped my way up the slope until almost to the place where I had left John.

Making my way by feel, I rounded a turn and started upward again when a strange rasping sound came to my ears. A few paces beyond, I found John. He lay on his side across the path; his breath came in whistling gasps. Bending over him, I searched for his wound and discovered an arrow protruding from his chest. How far it had entered I could not judge, nor had the time to determine. I only knew he still lived.

With all my strength, I lifted John and staggered up the path until my arms ached and my chest felt ready to burst. Yet I dared not stop to rest nor turn to look back, for the sound of the Romans moving more rapidly than I struck terror in my heart. Whether John still lived, I did not know. All that mattered was reaching the gate before the Romans reached me.

I remember nothing more of that climb, except that there came a time when it seemed I could not take another step, but forced myself to take ten more. And then nine more. Then eight, and finally, one and one and one. And I was sobbing and gasping for breath when, unexpectedly, I felt hands pry John from my arms. And with my last strength I blurted, "Take care — the arrow in him!" And then I remember no more.

Chapter XVIII

When I revived, someone was lifting my head and allowing wine to slowly trickle down my throat. I swallowed and gagged, and could not, for the moment, place my whereabouts. Eventually my head cleared, and I recognized my mother leaning over me. And then it all came back — Aram and Sara, the interminable climb with John. My mother gazed at me with deep concern and love. *She did not know!* She did not know.

The room seemed a confusion of people. A table had been drawn to the middle, and around it stood five or six people with oil lamps held aloft. Voices murmured indistinctly, and from the center of the commotion came the sounds of labored breathing.

I found the wash basin and plunged my head into the water, feeling the cold strike life into me like the slap of a hand. I began to sort out voices and faces — my father, Ananus ben Ezra, Rabbi Hillel, and two other men I did not immediately recognize. Drawing closer to the table, I saw they had cut away John's clothes above the waist.

Ananus ben Ezra, looking ashen, leaned on the table, feebly delivering instructions.

"Turn him gently," he said, "so I can examine his back."

I moved to a position opposite the physician and watched as they carefully shifted John. Blood had pooled at his back and dried there. One of the helpers wrung out a cloth and washed the back until I could see that the arrow had not come through.

A small swelling showed near the shoulder. Ananus touched the lump and the surrounding area, then looked across the table to me. "The arrow is between the ribs, which is good, but the blood is frothy . . ." Suddenly Ananus ben Ezra turned away. His whole body seemed to shrink into itself as he fought to control a paroxysm of coughing. My father, being nearest, led him to the couch. There the physician sat, head drooped between his knees.

No one spoke. The rabbi glanced at John, then at me. "I have had some experience as a physician," he said apologetically, "but not in surgery. You must do this, Simon. I cannot."

Alert now, I knew that without immediate treatment, John would surely die. I could not let that happen. I moved to the space Ananus ben Ezra had vacated and repeated the examination of John's back. The arrow point could not be more than a thumb's length from breaking through. The frothy blood meant, as I had learned, a punctured lung. John did not spit up much blood, and the wound only oozed, so I assumed no major vessel had been severed. Placing my hands over my face and closing my eyes, I blocked out everything but the pages of instruction I had read in one of ben Ezra's books. In his early years of study at Alexandria, he had meticulously copied the opinions of both Hippocrates and Celsus on the extraction of weapons. These he had insisted I study and commit to memory. I recalled the warning to ascertain what kind of weapon was lodged the body, for treatment depended on knowing precisely the properties of the arrow. I saw the page as though it were open before me now:

Warlike instruments differ from one another in material, figure, size, number, mode, and power.

In material, shafts may be made of wood or reeds, and the heads of iron, copper, tin, lead, horn, glass, bone, wood, or reeds.

In figure, some are round, some angled, some pointed and lance-shaped with three points, some are barbed and some without barbs. Of those barbed, the barbs may be pointed forward or backward, some diverging in opposite directions, so that whether pulled or pushed they may fasten in the body more firmly.

They differ in size, inasmuch as some are three fingers' breadth in size, and some as small as one finger.

In number, some are simple and some compounded. Of those compounded, small pieces of iron may be inserted in them, which in the extraction of the weapon remain concealed in deep-seated parts.

In mode, they differ as to how they are attached to the shaft, for some are inserted carelessly, so they will separate from the shaft and remain in the body when the shaft is extracted.

In power, some are poisoned, and some are not.

The most immediate decision to make was whether to pull the weapon back or push it forward. John's life depended on the choice. The construction of Roman arrows was familiar to me. I had assisted Ananus ben Ezra in extracting one from the leg of a soldier. The shafts were of wood, and fixed to the heads in such a manner that they might separate were the arrow withdrawn. The heads, of iron, were broad at the base and three-sided, each edge as sharp as a well-honed knife. To pull the arrow backward, against its path, posed added risk — damage to the flesh — and the possibility that the arrow head would remain behind. There were recorded instances of arrowheads remaining inside a victim as long as seven years without causing distress, and then suddenly being expelled from a part of the body remote from where first lodged. But this was unique and not to be counted on.

"Hold him very still," I directed. "I will try to push it through."

"Do you think that wise?" the rabbi asked sharply.

"If John dies because of you . . ." My father's voice trailed off.

And then I realized what they feared: that my decisions might be influenced by jealousy and hate.

"It is my fault that John is wounded," I said to them quietly. "Had I not run down the hill when we heard Sara scream, John might not have been hit."

My mother gasped and cried out Aram's name.

"If I leave the arrow in, he will surely die," I said, "and even if I remove it — the lung is a vital organ . . ."

"Forgive me for doubting you," my father said.

We turned our attention back to John. The two men took positions close to John, prepared to hold his body against my pressure from the opposite side. I grasped the arrow firmly and pushed with all my might. John screamed and opened his eyes. His hands clenched against his chest, plucking at the skin as though they could tear the pain out.

"Give him a strap to bite on," I ordered, "and get his hands out of my way!"

A fresh spurt of dark, frothy blood spewed from the wound. I could feel the flesh resist, then give way to the pressure, until suddenly the arrow tore through his skin to the outside. John's eyes closed again, and tears streamed out of them. My mother tenderly washed his sweat-streaked face.

I asked the rabbi, "Can you remove the arrowhead without splintering the wood?"

He nodded and moved forward. Silently, and with great tenderness, he disengaged the arrowhead from its shaft, then stepped back.

"Now, be prepared to hold him as I draw it out," I said. "I do not want to cause undue pain."

The arrow had entered from below. I tried to appraise the angle so as to pull straight. Then, bracing myself, I grasped the shaft near the point of entry and pulled back steadily. At first it would not move but clung to the flesh, reluctant to part with it.

By now, my hands were covered with blood, and the shaft slippery with it. I felt terribly hot, yet my body shook as though cold. John was pale as death, his breathing labored and shallow. Once I thought it had stopped altogether. Would he survive?

"Help me!" I cried angrily. It seemed incredible that no one had recognized my need. Suddenly my father stood behind me, grasping my waist, pulling along with me, until finally I felt the shaft move, slowly, then rapidly, released by the flesh into my hands.

Though I was exhausted and numb, the sight of the gushing wound and the frightening whistle that shrieked through the hole renewed my energy. Dropping the repugnant shaft as though it were a live viper, I reached for the wash basin to remove the bloody lather on my hands. Then, with a stack of dry pledgets from the pile on Ananus ben Ezra's medicinal shelf, I returned to the table.

It would be a miracle if they could stop the bleeding, and I have never relied on miracles.

Even while stuffing the cloth pads into the wound and firmly applying cold, wet sponges to the outside, I considered the next steps to take. There were countless possibilities. Some physicians maintained that the best way to stop hemorrhages was to treat the wound with one part frankincense, one part aloe, applied upon the down of a hare. Yet Ananus favored another, more complex compound. Only last week I had seen him mix it, and in fact had myself employed it with good results.

Unable to leave John to prepare the medication, I appealed to the rabbi for help, instructing him each step of the way. While he boiled the compound, I changed the pledgets often, for they swelled with blood almost as soon as I placed them in the wound.

The styptic compound the rabbi brought to me had the consistency of mud, and I worked it as far into the wound as I dared. Again and again I replaced the medication, until at last the bleeding eased, and a thrombus began to form.

That John had survived thus far could only be owed to the strength of youth and the power of God. Still, it was too soon to hope. His face remained gray, and his pulse raced. His forehead burned with fever. With the utmost gentleness I sponged his cheeks and parched lips, and carefully dripped water onto his tongue.

For the first time since I had taken over from Ananus ben Ezra, I glanced around. The two men who helped earlier had left. My mother slumped in a chair nearby.

Ben Ezra and my father were nowhere to be seen. Rabbi Hillel quietly recited his morning prayers.

The door to the outside opened, letting in a light that momentarily blinded me, and a figure entered. When my eyes focused again, I recognized Salome, the physician's daughter, looking alert and fresh.

"I have come to relieve you, Simon," she said, going to John's side and studying him with anxious concern. "How is he?"

"He sleeps now," I replied, suddenly feeling the fatigue of the long night. "How is your father?"

"Resting in your parents' rooms. My mother is with him. You must get some rest now. Go. I will call you if there is any change."

But I could not leave just yet. I watched Salome move to the basins, which she emptied and scrubbed, then re-filled with fresh water. She looked at the bloody shaft on the floor, then picked it up and tossed it into the cooking fire.

Within a short time, she had washed the floor, put the room in order, and begun cooking a good-smelling soup. Her movement about the room seemed so natural, so reassuring, that I began to feel refreshed, even hopeful. Salome had changed in these last months. No more the plump, awkward child I had met when I first came to apprentice. Now her motions were sure and fluid, full of grace. She no longer blushed when I spoke to her; instead, her direct gaze often tied my tongue.

When she caught me watching, Salome smiled with a hint of her old shyness and came to my side. "Let me take over now, Simon," she said. "What do you think? Will he live?"

"If he can last the day, there is a chance. The thrombus

must be bathed in wine to keep down the infection. And if it becomes inflamed, use oil," I said.

"Well then, I will do that while you eat and rest. Go." She gave me a gentle push.

"I will be just outside if you need me," I said, opening the door to the morning, to the sharp, invigorating air. It was still early, and few people walked about yet. The ground lay damp and sweet-smelling from the rain of the night before. Yellow and orange flowers, which had sprung up in the depressions on the plateau where the water collected, were beginning to open to the light. A south wind tossed the last leaves off the pomegranate trees.

I dug my knuckles into my burning eyes and let myself ponder for a moment Aram and Sara's fate, John's chances for recovery, our very future here — if we had one. And then I raised my arms to the wide sky and smiled. Despite all, how good to be alive!

Chapter XIX

The messenger from Marius's camp appeared highly excited. After he saluted and received my permission to speak, he said that Marius had captured two Jews trying to escape and was keeping them under heavy guard.

"Why does he not bring them here?" I asked, annoyed.

"I was told the Commander would understand why he could not leave the eastern sector," he replied. "Patrols are out even now searching for others who might have broken through our lines."

I grunted. Marius was determined to prove himself capable, to regain my respect and win back my approval. But I despised the theatricality of this little show. Did he expect that I would ride out to his camp myself?

To the messenger I said, "Tell Marius that he is to report to me with the captives as soon as he has determined the extent of the escape. In his absence, he is to give temporary command to Calvarius. Tell him also that

I congratulate him on his alertness and his admirable attention to duty."

The messenger saluted and withdrew.

It was early morning before Marius appeared with the two prisoners under guard behind him. He looked as if he had only recently bathed and donned fresh cape and tunic, not as one who had been on horseback all night searching the hills for Jews. That he had taken the time to groom himself before reporting irritated me, for I saw in this the actor who comes upon the stage to the fanfare of trumpets, not the dedicated soldier.

He pushed before me two very frightened young people, a man of perhaps fifteen and a woman-child. Their faces were streaked with dirt, and their clothes torn. The shawl that I have seen the male Jews wear over their heads as a symbol of respect to their god had been used as a rope to tie the man's hands behind his back.

When Marius related the circumstances of their capture, I could not help but admire his thoroughness. From the first day that he had been sent to command the eastern defenses, he had instituted a unique guard system. The circumvallation wall was lightly defended, but a short ways beyond, guards stood duty in radial lines, about fifty paces apart, all the way to the sea. These guards took their positions as soon as it became too dark for the Jews above to see the formation, and withdrew before first light. It seems the two prisoners had been moving north, then reversed direction when they perceived the line of guards blocking their progress. But they were caught like fish in a net, for the next line of guards captured them a short distance beyond.

"Have you interrogated them?" I asked Marius.

"Briefly," he replied. "I thought you would wish to do that. There is one thing strange. They seem to under-

146

stand Aramaic when it is spoken, but they respond only in the Hebrew tongue."

"What did you find on their persons?"

"Each carried a small pack. They held nothing of significance — no maps, no messages. Only dried foodstuffs, a few articles of clothing, and some coins."

"Send for the prisoner Ananias, then, and bring these two into my tent when he arrives," I ordered.

What I relate now of the interview is of necessity a secondhand account, for the answers to my questions came through the prisoner. Whether he related all that the young Jews told him, or even exactly what they said, I cannot be sure, for the first part of the interrogation was in the Israelite tongue.

I learned that the two were Aram ben Eleazar and Sara, his wife, attempting to escape through our lines to reach help in Damascus for their people. No others had left Masada but them. There were about a thousand Jews on the rock. They claimed these Zealots had plentiful water and adequate food and weapons.

"Ask them," I said with sudden inspiration, "why their leader sent them on this mission when they can speak only the Jews' language? How did they expect to negotiate in the cities without knowing the language of the region?"

Ananias translated my question, but it became obvious that the young man and the girl clearly understood my words, and they lowered their heads.

Speaking directly to the man, I ordered, "You will answer my questions in Aramaic now, and waste no more of my time. If you do not, I will take your woman and have her whipped before your eyes — until she is dead."

This brought a look of horror to the girl's eyes and a glare of hatred from her husband. However, it achieved my purpose. The succeeding questions and answers no longer required the services of Ananias.

"Now, you will tell me why you were sent on this mission," I said. "I do not believe this fabrication that you seek help against our armies. Just what did you hope to achieve?" Suddenly I had another inspiration. I walked closer to the young man. "Your name is ben Eleazar?"

The young man nodded.

"Son of Eleazar — Eleazar ben Ya'ir?"

His wife's eyes, widening in alarm, told me all I wanted to know. "How very interesting," I said, turning to Marius.

"How *very* interesting," Marius repeated. "So, Eleazar uses his position to save his own family!"

"Clearly honor is not an Israelite trait," I agreed.

The young man stiffened. "We were not sent to be saved. You are wrong!" he cried.

Marius thought this very amusing. After he had enjoyed a good laugh, I said, "You expect me to believe you were sent to get reinforcements? How stupid are you? Do you know how long it will be before we are at your walls? A matter of weeks. Do you think you could have organized an army in that time?"

The man glanced quickly at his wife, then with patience and dignity stated, "We were not sent to save those on Masada. Nor to save ourselves."

His wife watched him with great attention. Something in his manner reached Marius, and his amusement dissolved. "Then why were you sent?" I asked.

"We want our people everywhere to know that we are not cutthroats and cowards, as the traitor Josephus says of us. We fight for our freedom."

Marius laughed scornfully. "Freedom! An honorable purpose indeed." He turned to me. "How often have we heard those words before — from how many defeated nations? Every people since the beginning of time has claimed they fought for that prize. But in the end, do you know who captures it?" He pressed a hand to his chest. "The best organized. The most powerful! And here is another truth to swallow." Marius paused dramatically, savoring the rapt attention of the prisoners. "It is the victor who writes history!"

The young man stared at Marius in disbelief. He looked to the Jew Ananias, who averted his eyes. He searched my face for support. But I revealed nothing. I believed, as Marius, in this truth.

With childlike stubbornness, he said, "It could not be that all these years of bloodshed and sacrifice will go down in history as villainy. If that were true . . ."

"If that were true?" I asked.

"Then the Lord would make us the victors, for we have righteousness on our side."

Unbelievable — to retain faith against such odds! Their entire country was under our thumb. That we would break through their defenses was only a question of time. Even Ananias recognized the inevitability of their defeat. I could see it in his pinched, tight lips, in his hollow cheeks, in his dead eyes. But not in the faces of the two before me. Suddenly their unreasonable stubbornness became insufferable. In the face of their certainty, I felt vulnerable and foolish for having given them so long an audience.

"Take them away," I told Marius. "Tie them to posts, in full view of their people above. Assemble all the Jewish prisoners, that they too may see how we treat those who oppose us. We will see how powerful their god can be."

"What will you do with us?" the young man asked.

He looked from me to Marius, and when neither of us spoke, to Ananias. Ananias looked away.

"I see," the young man said, squaring his shoulders. His eyes sought mine, imploring. "Spare my wife! In all her life she has never done a cruel or unkind thing. Please! I beg you!"

The girl strained against her bonds, trying to draw closer to her husband. "Aram! Do not beg him!" she cried. But the young man's eyes remained fixed on mine.

"Take them away," I commanded, turning back to the table where my breakfast waited. What were these two compared to the men in my command who had been killed and burned during the surprise raid? What were they, in terms of the months of effort this siege was taking? *Nothing.*

Unless — unless they could be put to use. But how?

As I drank the watered wine, washing down the monotonous gruel of pulse and honey, I considered how these two might work for us, then recalled an interesting story. In the early years of this war, Titus had taken a Galilean fortress. He had captured the leader and was preparing to crucify him when the besieged unexpectedly capitulated, unable to witness the death of their beloved leader in such a fashion.

How much did these two young people mean to Eleazar ben Ya'ir? To the people of Masada?

BY MIDDAY, the sun had steamed the moisture from the earth. The air became clear and crisp. Hundreds of prisoners, laboring under leather shields, were on the ramp. Even though the assault embankment will be much like an arrowhead in shape, we offer a narrow front to the enemy. Indeed, they have persistently tried to hinder our progress, but our bowmen direct their arrows so steadily at the besieged on the wall, any counterpressure from them has been ineffective.

We are making good progress on the ramp. It measures now a solid 330 feet in height, but is still not sufficiently high for the use of the siege machine. It will be two months — more, perhaps — before we can begin any serious attack from its summit.

I ordered the two captives bound back to back at the base of the embankment so that our Jewish prisoners who were bringing up sand or rocks or lumber would have to pass them, and the Zealots above might have a good view. They were given neither food nor water during the day, and when one of the slaves broke rank and tried to give the girl a drink from his flask, he was summarily whipped. Eventually the Jewish prisoners could not bear to look in their direction, and filed by shamefaced.

Late in the day, the guards piled faggots at the feet of the hostages. Then, with the tribune Sabinus at my side, I stood before the two and addressed myself to the Zealot leader.

"Eleazar ben Ya'ir," I called, and my voice resounded so clearly I had no doubt it would be heard above.

After a short wait, a voice returned, "I am Eleazar."

"These hostages are of your family. Your son and his wife. Do you acknowledge them?"

"I do," he replied.

"Then hear me well. They will die this day unless you surrender Masada to me at once."

A murmur of many voices came from above; almost immediately, the reply came: "What is their fate if we surrender?"

"They take their chances with the others — in the arena," I answered.

"Then we will leave them to God," Eleazar ben Ya'ir replied with finality in his voice.

I waited a moment for other words, but none came. Turning to the tribune, I gave the command. Immediately he stepped forward, lowered his torch, and ignited the dry faggots at the prisoners' feet. The girl screamed. Her husband gazed skyward, eyes dark with fear, lips moving.

Then, while the flames licked at their feet and tested their clothes, a strange hum that grew to a babble filled the air. From the lips of the Zealots above and the prisoners below came the lamentations and prayers of the Israelites, rising feverishly in agonized chorus, until even the cries of the dying were swallowed up in it.

Chapter XX

Salome became my only contact with the world beyond our walls that first day after the operation. I would sleep in snatches while she watched over John. Then, silent and preoccupied, she would cook or clean while I stood vigil over John. Afterward, she would leave to learn what she could of Aram and Sara's fate. Ananus ben Ezra lay spent in the next room, too ill to offer advice or assistance.

It was Salome who anxiously described to me how my brother and Sara were bound to a cross at the base of the ramp, and who told me with growing agitation as the day wore on of the faggots piled at their feet.

"What does it mean?" she cried, knowing, but hoping I would tell her differently.

She came running to me late in the afternoon, lips trembling, eyes wide with horror, unable to speak.

"What is it, Salome?" I demanded almost harshly, rising and shaking her shoulders, and knowing what she must say.

"Simon . . ." she pleaded, reaching out for solace. But I could offer none.

The knowledge of what must happen to Sara and Aram had shadowed me all day like death. As I stared down at John hour after hour, I saw not his fevered face but the Roman soldiers in rows on the plain below, the Jewish prisoners, tattered and huddled together in mutual misery, and in the center of it all — Aram and Sara. I rubbed my eyes to dispel the vision, but even behind closed lids I saw them — terrified, uncomprehending, reaching out to me. Now I could not push the vision away, for it was true.

Why had it not been me or John? We had experienced brutality and violence — even death. But Sara. And Aram! They were innocents, unschooled in hatred. I beat my fists against the wall, wanting to share in their pain. The cries of my brother rang in my ears, tore at my heart. Aram! I can do nothing. Nothing! Oh Lord, nothing.

WHEN SALOME told me what had transpired between my father and the Roman commander, I felt both bitterness and reluctant pride. Eleazar knowingly committed Aram and Sara to death. What a terrible decision to make! Many would condemn him for it, calling him heartless and cold. If he could sentence his own son, then he could as well see us all dead. Yet, in my despair, I admired him. Little courage is needed to lead a cause that might end in death when death seems unlikely, but to lead a cause almost certain to end in death, to follow it to the end, takes the kind of courage and integrity few men have.

This was a time I longed to be with my parents to share my sorrow, to offer comfort and moral support, to grieve with them. But with John so precariously balanced

154

between life and death, I could not leave him, and my parents visited only briefly, understanding this.

The thrombus that had formed at the entrance to the wound had swollen. Now it hung like a ripe fruit, angry red in color, throbbing with each pulse. Worse yet, its base appeared white, as though bloated with pus. John churned restlessly on the table that Salome had converted to a bed. Sometimes he cried out in anguished bursts of meaningless words; sometimes he cried out for Deborah.

I had sent word of John's condition to Deborah, and she received the news badly. She begged to see him, but I urged her to stay away until the crisis passed.

For most of the second night, Salome and I took turns bathing the thrombus with wine and sponging John's head and body to reduce the fever, hoping always that the swelling would be absorbed, at least enough to suggest the start of healing. But it only grew uglier. By morning I decided that the sac of blood must be lanced to release the dangerous infection that seemed to be spreading.

Salome appeared tired from the long strain. I myself felt numb with fatigue and sorrow, but when I told her of my plans and the help I would need, she immediately went to find Rabbi Hillel.

Even after I splashed cold water over my eyes, they still burned, and holding the pointed probe steady would take all my powers of concentration. While the rabbi prepared the searing iron on the cooking stone, mumbling prayers as he waited for it to heat, Salome stood by with a shallow pan to catch the blood.

Before me, my friend lay helpless, feverish, struggling for life. His cracked lips parted; his tongue sought water. His eyes were sunken in their inflamed sockets, and the wine he swallowed to ease the pain dribbled down his chin. As I held the probe above the thrombus, the enormity of my responsibility struck me as it had not in the immediacy of removing the arrow. Life or death lay in my hands; whatever I had learned of medicine would be tested now. If I failed to save John, I would fail Ananus ben Ezra, Deborah, and most of all, myself.

I raised the gleaming probe to the light, examining it dispassionately: this blade, this weapon, this instrument that the Lord would guide my hand to use. Suddenly, fatigue, hesitancy, and self-doubt all vanished. My eyes cleared; my mind knew peace; my hand felt strength and purpose.

With a quick, sure stroke, I slashed the inflamed thrombus so that the dark red blood spurted forth into the pan. Then I gently forced the infection to the surface and sponged the wound clean with wine-soaked pledgets. As the bleeding slowed, Rabbi Hillel came forward and placed the searing iron on the open wound. The acrid smell of burning flesh filled the room, and a weak cry came from John. But the iron did its work. When he removed it, no blood issued from the blackened flesh around the wound.

The next day John opened his eyes and seemed aware for the first time since the operation. He smiled wanly and asked for water, then slept deeply. When he woke again, his fever seemed to be abating. Rabbi Hillel and Salome's mother took turns bathing the seared skin with oil while I rested. In the evening, after I had checked his pulse and felt his head, and examined his chest and back wounds, there was reason to hope. Calling Rabbi Hillel to the table, I asked his opinion. He pressed an ear to John's chest, peered thoughtfully at his eyes and skin, and nodded. "Yesterday I was certain he could not live," he said solemnly. "It is a miracle."

Salome, folding pledgets nearby, interrupted. With

unaccustomed spirit she protested, "Simon is a fine physician, Rabbi Hillel, perhaps as good even as my father. It was his skill and knowledge that saved John — not a miracle."

The rabbi regarded her. His understanding glance toward me and then his gentle smile for Salome brought confusion and color to her face. "Never forget the Lord's part, my dear," he said, placing a hand on her shoulder.

"And do not forget Salome's part." I spoke directly to her. "A better assistant I could not have found had I searched the whole of the Roman Empire."

Salome's deep blue eyes, so like her father's, met mine. The affection I felt for this kind and gentle girl must have shown in my look, for her face broke into a sudden brilliant smile. And this time it was I who felt confused and turned away.

Though John was young and strong, his wound healed slowly. For days his recovery remained in doubt. During this time, Deborah spent many hours with him. She arrived early each morning with a small bouquet of flowers or a plate of nuts and dried fruit. She sat tensely at John's side, hour after hour, watching him. Whatever doubts or fears she once had about his character seemed, at least temporarily, replaced by concern for his health.

One day, when John was well enough to be aware of her presence, he asked after Aram and Sara. "Did the Romans . . . ?" he whispered weakly, watching Deborah. Tears filled her eyes, and she nodded. As a sob tore from his throat, John clutched his painful wound. He turned his head to the wall and would not speak again.

When John grew stronger, Deborah came to feed him and speak quietly of hopeful things — of the farm they would have in the Galilee some day, of the people who constantly asked after him, and of the wedding date they

157

must set. John's eyes never left her face. In her absence, he grew restless and lost.

Though many opportunities arose for Deborah and me to speak during those days, we found little to say to each other. She seemed as absorbed in John's recovery as if her own life depended on it.

One morning, when she caught me staring at the two of them, her look of concern changed, and for the first time in a long while her eyes focused on me.

"You have been very far away," I said.

She smiled distractedly. "Will he get well?"

"Yes, Deborah." I searched her face for some small sign that she might yet care for me.

"Truly?" she asked, as if not daring hope for such an answer. Her hands flew to her cheeks in disbelief. "Truly?"

"Truly," I responded, surprised to find that though her eyes held nothing for me, it no longer mattered.

"Oh, Simon!" she exclaimed. "I promised God that if John lived, I would never again doubt . . ."

I understood. If John lived, she would never again doubt that she loved him.

"It will be all right, Deborah," I said, trying to heal the awkwardness between us.

I wanted to believe my words. Aram and Sara's loss still hurt deeply, but I had much to be grateful for. For satisfying, purposeful work. For each day of life. For Salome, whom I would ask to be my wife. And for faith, no matter how unfounded, that somehow we would survive the Roman siege.

Chapter XXI

For days I had been so occupied with caring for John that what occurred beyond the walls of his room seemed no longer my concern. The few times I did break away, I visited my mother and father and Sara's parents, who mourned deeply for their children. The fact that John would live lightened their hearts only briefly.

Sara's parents took it particularly hard. "How could it be?" her mother asked constantly, as if placing blame. "Eleazar himself assured us Sara would be all right."

Her father, always a talkative man before, became mute. When he broke his silence, after many days, it was to ask a stranger, "Do you know of my daughter, Sara?" Before the man could answer, he continued, "Did you hear the good news? She is safely in Damascus now." The stranger stood openmouthed, as if to protest, but Sara's father would not pause to allow contradiction. He had found a way, at last, to live with his sorrow.

When I realized that John would live, I took interest again in activities outside my physician's duties. Every day I sought time to visit the western wall to observe the progress on the assault ramp.

In only the short while that I had been too preoccupied to visit, an enormous change had taken place. It appeared the Romans intended to raise the ramp to the level of our walls! Though we continued to roll rocks down on the workers, the embankment grew higher and wider daily. Nothing could be done to prevent it. Even night raids to the Roman camps accomplished little beyond harassment. Worse, we could not undo by night what thousands of prisoners built by day.

The fact that the Romans slowly but surely gained ground came clearest to us all with the loss of the western cisterns. Their capture announced the enemy's nearness, though the loss of water would not actually affect us until the dry season. We still had access to the cisterns on the southeast, and those on the plateau were full from recent rains.

Nevertheless, conservation became essential. Water rations were at once reduced. Women, fearing their families would die of thirst, gathered at the cisterns on our plateau before the appointed time each day to collect their quota. Soldiers in the Roman camp on the hill overlooking our plateau fired at these groups, perhaps believing we were close to the end of our resources.

Realizing that the Romans rejoiced over the cistern capture and must consider us as good as dead from thirst, my father called his men together one day and gave a strange order.

"Remove your outer garments and saturate them with water," he said solemnly. "Then hang them, dripping wet, from the battlements."

For a moment the men seemed perplexed, thinking perhaps that my father had broken under the strain.

"But Eleazar," a man asked, "why waste water thus?"

"They think us dying of thirst," my father grinned.

As his purpose came clear, murmurs, then smiles and chuckles ensued. Soon all rushed to do his bidding.

"By Jupiter!" someone joked, imitating his notion of a Roman commander. "And I thought those Israelites must be as dry as parchment by now! Wherever does all that water come from?" Welcome laughter followed his words, heartier than the remark deserved.

"Did you not know," another continued in his version of a Roman soldier, "that the rock of Masada is really hollow, and the Jews have dug shafts to the center, which is full of water?"

A high-pitched voice complained, "While we poor souls must travel many furlongs for a drink . . ."

When all had done as my father directed, the whole wall ran with water, and though an extravagant waste, it was a short-lived victory we could all appreciate.

Laughter, however brief, relieved the grimness of our plight. We took satisfaction in knowing that we Jews — less than a thousand strong — had been able to hold off the entire Tenth Legion longer than any other besieged fortress. In a small way, we were like David against Goliath, except that the Roman army was infinitely more powerful than that great giant.

And their power grew. One fresh spring day, when the desert bloomed with yellow flowers and new lambs frollicked on the plateau, ramp construction ceased. The cone-shaped ramp was now quite broad at the summit — some four hundred cubits, I judged — and only forty cubits below our wall. On this broad base, the enemy began to hoist large rectangular stones and to lay them in the shape of a platform. It became obvious that the new construction would make it possible for them to concentrate their firing power directly into our fortress. We had to prevent this construction at any cost.

But how? The builders carried leather shields, and rocks bounced off them like raindrops. Meanwhile, dozens of projectile throwers bombarded the men on our wall. In synchronized barrage, catapults shot lances into the air, stone throwers hurled rocks weighing half a hundredweight, and archers fired a dense shower of arrows.

To remain within range of such fire power invited death. Yet our forces fought from the towers and even the exposed ramparts, pouring boiling oil on those who tried to scale our wall. The noise of battle — the sharp whistle of stones and arrows and the screams of the wounded — went on without relief through the daylight hours. Women and children escaped to safety indoors, covering their ears.

I could no longer serve at the battlements, for now I gave all my time to the wounded — men who had lost an arm or leg, men who had been pierced by arrows, a dying woman who had been struck by a rock with such force that her unborn child had been torn from her belly and hurled many feet away. Horrible. Horrible. I could not keep up with the carnage.

Despite all efforts to slow its progress, the platform grew, grew until it reached almost to the top of our wall — a substantial structure, at least fifty cubits square. When the platform was completed, an even more terrifying structure grew from it.

The new structure became a tower, plated all over with iron so we could not set it afire. It seemed to spring from the platform like a huge and hideous plant. Though we hindered its progress, even making daylight raids against the working parties and the soldiers at the machines, eventually it stood sixty cubits higher than the platform, and from its protection men could look down and fire onto our plateau.

We found no surcease from their attack now. From their iron-plated tower came darts and stones shot with hideous accuracy. From the platform came an endless barrage of arrows, javelins, and stones catapulted and hurled at us.

Everywhere the stench of blood and death hung in the air. Ananus ben Ezra's three rooms became a hospital to which the wounded and dying were brought. The physician, himself very ill, nevertheless dragged about from patient to patient, catching sleep in snatches, as I did, only to be instantly awakened by new patients carried in, or sudden cries of pain.

I had learned to recognize those who would benefit from medical attention and those beyond it. One day a soldier, younger even than Aram, was brought to me by two men who were at his side when he was struck by a javelin. His wound was as serious as John's had been, and at a different time I might have saved him.

"I cannot help him," I told the pair, sickened at having to make this choice. "Find Rabbi Hillel. Perhaps he can help." My eyes quickly assessed four other men awaiting treatment, and I moved to the one in greatest need.

"What do you mean?" one of the men challenged harshly, grabbing my arm.

I shrugged out of his grasp and started to remove the blood-stained tunic of the patient. "It would take hours to treat him, and he would likely die anyway. Meanwhile, others would certainly die because I could not reach them soon enough."

"But you saved John! And he was no less mortally wounded!" the man protested. "Do you not take an oath as a physician? To help all who need help?"

"Please remove him. I must help those who might be able to fight again."

"You play God!" the man accused, following me.

I did not respond, my mind already absorbed in treating the wounded man before me.

"You *must* help him. Look at him!"

Glancing at the dying boy, I felt a wave of self-disgust, and a knot of tears grew in my chest. "Salome, prepare an opiate for him," I instructed. "It will at least ease the pain."

"Oh . . . my God . . ." the man moaned, standing helplessly in the middle of the room.

How callous, to rule one man might live and another must die! If there ever came a respite from this slaughter, a moment when I might reflect on what it all meant, I would be revolted by what now seemed logical and justified.

NEWS OF THE conflict reached me in snatches through my patients and through those who brought them.

"How can we fight those we cannot see? They are firing from slits in that iron tower now!" one frantic soldier cried.

"Rabbi Hillel has asked for help in burying the sacred scrolls . . ."

". . . John came to the battlements today. He is thin and pale, but his presence gave us hope."

"Eleazar has ordered those who can be spared to strip the beams in the roof structure of Herod's palace. Everything wooden is being carried to the western wall."

"Why?" I asked, distracted from my patient momentarily. "What does he want with so much wood?"

"We are constructing two walls of wood, with sand between."

"Why?" I wondered, considering the possibilities.

"He says the Romans will bring up the ram now that the platform and tower are completed."

"The battering ram?" I asked, startled.

"Yes. That is why their firing cover has become so heavy."

That is why we have so many wounded, I thought, suddenly filled with fear.

I WRITE THESE words in a dim light, hurriedly and sick at heart. And I think — time grows short.

Chapter XXII

We have been occupied here for more than seven months!

Twenty thousand people against a mere thousand stubborn Jews. How that rankles! Will Vespasian understand such dalliance? He himself took similar fortresses in the Galilee in only a month's time. Yet, could I have done anything different? The geography, the elements, the surprise attack on our camps — all contributed to delays.

When I take Masada, it will hardly appear an achievement. Can I redeem myself? Take prisoners? If I could bring to Rome the insurgents from this last Judean fortress, perhaps *then* the time wasted here will be forgotten. I can see it now. I will march my captives, just as Vespasian and Titus did, all the way from Ostia, down the Appian Way, to the Senate. And I will present these remnants of a conquered nation to my Caesar.

The end is near. The embankment is finished. The platform that rises to the level of their walls is done. The iron tower, from which our men can safely fire into their fortress, is complete. All day, artillery squads stationed on the summit of the ramp operate their quick-firing arrow catapults; and the machines hurl their missiles into the fortress. Any Jews who dare leave cover, or are fool-hardy enough to try to interfere with our operations, do not last.

And now it was time for the battering ram. And for this, I had to recall Marius.

It was a difficult decision to make, and I had many reservations even after the orders were on their way, but I saw no other choice. Cestius, whose knowledge of the ram I had depended on, was wounded while directing the tower construction. Others knew how to operate the machine, but none with his experience — except Marius. Though I would never trust Marius again with large-scale decisions, I needed him now. Personal animosity had to be put aside for the benefit of this final phase of the siege.

Marius was wary of me now, watchful, like an animal who stalks its prey, uncertain where to attack. He was insolent too, as though he knew he had the upper hand because I needed him. I wondered if he suspected that I have been writing these notes about our encounters and that I will use them against him when the time comes.

"It is unfortunate you lost so much time because of the rains," he said smoothly when we met again. "Of course the engineers should have shored up the slope in anticipation of slippage. Did you not want to be back in Caesarea by March?" he clucked maliciously.

I saw no purpose in rising to his bait. Our personal feud would wait. I had to get that ram into operation. I was determined to bring this endless siege to conclusion.

"We are ready to bring up the ram, Marius. I brought you here because Cestius is confined to his tent, and we must have an experienced man in charge."

"So . . . you need me now," he said with a knowing smile. "Before, I was not good enough to keep around. Tell me, why should I risk my neck now to save your reputation?"

A familiar pain shot through my belly. "It is your duty as a Roman officer to obey my commands," I said in measured tones. "If you do not, be sure that your insubordination will be brought to the attention of Vespasian himself."

"What have I to lose? My rank? You already intend to blame the surprise raid on me. But — when this is brought before the Court of Justice, we will see who is held responsible. Rome has conquered whole nations in the time it has taken to lay siege to this — this anthill."

I could no longer control my rage. "Will you take charge of the battering ram, or shall I have you put in chains?" I clutched my stomach as the pain bit from within.

Marius shrugged, unperturbed by my outburst, coldly appraising my discomfort. "Very well, General Silva," he said with an exaggerated salute. "I will do as you order. But your day will come. And when it does — remember: the men are with me!"

Within hours, Marius had the battering ram rolled up the embankment to the tower — no small feat. For it was a complex and cumbersome machine. The ram itself was a huge wooden beam like the mast of a ship, fitted at the end with a great lump of iron in the shape of a ram's head. This device was more advanced than those first used in the war; it had been improved with each use, first by Vespasian and then by Titus, his son.

The ram lay in a cradle of leather loops slung from a large scaffold, and was operated by men protected from

168

the enemy's fire by a heavy wooden roof. Above the roof were additional catapult mountings.

To watch the ram in operation is inspiring. It is drawn back by a great number of men who then swing it forward with a gigantic heave, legs moving like those of an enormous centipede, forward, forward, until the projecting ram head meets the stone of the wall. Then, still in control of the rope that attaches to the ram, they run backward, and backward, until the beam has reached the origin of its swing.

Once the ram was in operation, I returned to my tent, for the pains in my stomach had become intolerable. "Avoid anger," the legion medicos had advised, and I had laughed. "You may as well tell me to avoid breathing," I had said. Only drugs eased the pain at times, but these made me lightheaded and dull.

I had fallen asleep to the slam of the ram against the fortress wall, leaving instructions to be roused as soon as a breach was made. But suddenly I awakened to the certainty that something was wrong.

Instead of the regular crunch of iron against rock, there sounded a dull thud, then a long pause and shouted orders, and confusion.

"What is it?" I asked the nearest soldier as I ran from my tent.

"They have hung bags of chaff from the walls!" he exclaimed angrily. "When the ram strikes, it hits the bags, and the blow is cushioned or deflected."

This was no surprise. Others had countered the ram in this manner before. There were various ways to retaliate. I mounted my horse to ride to the action, knowing Marius would probably employ reap hooks to cut away the bags, and the ram would be back in action within the hour.

As I reached the platform, the ram was drawn forward again. But instead of using reap hooks, Marius had devised a quicker method. A single soldier sat atop the ram, his legs gripping the wood like the flanks of a horse. When the beam reached the wall and was held there by the straining efforts of those who controlled it, the soldier reached up with his sword and slashed the ropes holding the bags of chaff.

Suddenly and unexpectedly, a Zealot soldier appeared above, and with the coolness of a woman emptying her laundry water, dumped a stream of boiling oil on our soldier. Almost simultaneously the Zealot fell, struck by a Roman arrow, while our man tumbled from the ram, screaming in agony.

Again the ram ceased for a time, but eventually moved forward again, another soldier riding its head. This time, as soon as a Zealot appeared on the wall, a hundred arrows flew his way. Soon the bags of chaff lay spilled on the slope below.

I felt great satisfaction as the ram continued its relentless hammering at the sturdy block wall. Hour after hour it pounded the wall. Finally the first block broke away, and then the next — the breach was made.

A long, loud, jubilant yell rang out from our men below. The months of sand and heat, of short water rations, of routine and boredom, of harassment from the enemy, were over. Masada was ours for the taking.

As the ram continued to pound at the wall to enlarge the breach, Marius, head tilted as though listening acutely, moved from one side of the tower to the other, and finally disappeared inside it.

When he emerged, he came directly to me.

"Something is wrong," he said. "The ram has broken through, but it does not sound right."

"What do you think it is?"

"I do not know. I thought I could tell by looking from the tower, but the angle of view does not allow me to see what lies immediately beyond on the plateau."

"Perhaps the wall is thicker than we supposed, or the ram is striking too much debris. Send in a crew to clear the way so the breach will be more passable."

He nodded, abstracted. "Perhaps so. Perhaps it is only debris."

But he had planted doubt in my mind. From that point on my eyes strained to see through the dust, stirred up by the crumbling wall, to what lay beyond.

The answer came soon enough. Prisoners, clearing away rocks to enlarge the breach, suddenly streamed out of it.

"Have they finished?" I demanded of the cohort commander in charge.

"No, commander," he replied. "They have broken through the rock, but there is a wooden wall beyond which they cannot penetrate."

"So that was it!" Marius exclaimed, angrily slamming his fist into his hand. "I should have known."

"To the ram!" Marius shouted, and he drove the men forward, pulling with them so as to smash the ram against the cursed inner wall.

After only a little while he came to me again.

"It should have fallen by now," he said. "Any wooden wall, no matter how well constructed, would have given way to that pummeling, unless . . ."

"Unless . . . ," I continued, "unless they have constructed a *double* wall of wood, with sand between. The sand compacts with each strike of the ram, making the wall even more sturdy."

"Yes," he hissed. "Clever Jews."

"Burn it down," I said, for Marius seemed unable to think beyond the battering ram. He nodded absently, staring up at the fortress wall.

The wind direction was in our favor — of that I made quite sure. Blowing, as usual, from the southwest, it would drive the flames inward toward the defenders. When I gave the command, a volley of flaming torches struck the wall. Being made mostly of wood, it caught fire, and owing to its loose construction, the whole thickness of it was soon ablaze.

Marius and I stood in the tower watching the conflagration, each of us engrossed in his own thoughts. This siege would soon be over. When the fire consumed the wall, we could march in and take the Zealot fortress and all its defenders. Some would certainly resist, but with our superior numbers we should quickly quell any opposition and come away with a good number of prisoners.

But my vision of victory was short-lived. In one of those freak climatic changes that characterize this part of the country, the wind shifted suddenly to the north. The flames that had been driving into the fortress turned on us.

In no time fire licked at the tower walls. Marius and I scrambled to escape as the heat became unbearable. There seemed no air to breathe. Soldiers leaped from the tower; fire engulfed the ram superstructure, the iron-plated tower, roaring with the fury of the gods . . .

Then, as if by divine providence, the fickle wind shifted again. The fire that had nearly destroyed everything we had built was flung against the Zealots' inner wall, turning it into one solid, blazing mass.

When order was again restored and the flames consuming the machines put out, I appraised the burning wall and declared, "Tonight we will keep watch, that none may escape. In the morning, we will take Masada."

Marius, face aglow with anticipation, indecent in its wild excitement, did not want to wait. It reminded me of the day we had first come upon Masada. "Now, Flavius, now! Why not now?" he demanded.

I would like to believe that my decision to delay until the morrow was based not on emotion but on logic. The wall still burned furiously. As a result of the fire, our men were spent and disorganized. Night was near. The Zealots could not escape. Only a burning wall separated me from them now. After seven months of careful planning and patience, what difference could a few more hours make?

"Tomorrow," I said again, raising one hand to stay Marius's renewed protest. "We will as *I* say. The Jews will be there still. Tomorrow we will take Masada."

Chapter XXIII

"All men to the wall!" I heard the cry in the operating room; moments later an old man opened the door and called, "Hurry! You are needed."

How shall I describe the scene at the ramparts? Even while the battering ram pounded the wall, our men stubbornly continued to pelt those who, under cover of their shields, swung the ram. But they were falling under the barrage of spears and stones slung at them. Struck by a stone, one of our men had his head knocked off, his skull flung like a pebble the length of our plateau.

Fearing surely that the Romans would be upon them at any moment, women and children huddled together, crying and praying. Their wails could be heard above the noise of the legion, above the battering of the ram, and above the scream of the arrows and stones rending the air. Afraid their lamentation might affect his men, John, still weak from his wounds, commanded they lock themselves in their rooms and hold their tongues.

People ran this way and that, disregarding the rain of arrows. Each thud of the battering ram became a spike driven into the heart. At the wooden wall, where men lay beams end to end while others hammered them in place, my father shouted, "Hurry, hurry! There is little time!"

Then, suddenly, the pounding ceased.

My father, face lined with fatigue, looked at me. Our eyes met in silent acknowledgment. "They are here — only paces away now — beyond this wall of wood and sand."

And then it began again, again, a dull, repeated thud against the wooden wall. Our fighting men stood shoulder to shoulder, spears at the ready, should the Romans burst through.

Although the battering continued, each time the ram met the quickly constructed inner wall it only compacted the sand between the frames. I took a deep breath and nearly smiled. Those around me cheered. But our joy faded as smoke soon filled our nostrils. And we saw great fingers of flame reaching skyward, blown into our fortress by the ever-present south winds.

Many fell to their knees and prayed. Even I silently begged God to spare us.

Suddenly, the flames that had been licking at the inner wall abated, as if a giant hand had stifled them. Screams of alarm and pain now came from the Roman side, and we realized that God had heard our pleas. He had turned the wind toward the enemy, blowing the flames out upon those who sought to destroy us!

Soldier hugged soldier. Men danced for joy. Tears streamed down faces. The terrible machines would be destroyed! We were saved! I looked about to see John leaning against the wall as if he might faint, and my father gazing up at the suddenly clear sky above.

The wind that now turned the flames from us brought the fragrance of pomegranates and figs. For a moment it seemed another time, another spring, and words from the songs of Solomon came to me:

> For lo, the winter is past, the rain is over and gone;
> The flowers appear on the earth;
> The time of the singing of birds is come, and the voice of
>   the turtle is heard in our land;
> The fig tree putteth forth her green figs, and the vines with
>   the tender grape give a good smell.

But soon, as suddenly as before, the wind shifted again, and the blue sky turned black with smoke, red with flames.

Chapter XXIV

It is dark. Yet the fires raging around me make it seem like day. I must wait now. And with what little time remains try to finish these writings, begun, so hopefully, only months ago.

When we realized the Romans would not attack until morning, my father gathered us together and said, "Long ago we resolved to serve neither the Romans nor anyone else but God. We must now prove our determination by our deeds. We have never submitted to slavery, even when it brought no danger with it. We must not choose slavery now.

"We were the first to revolt, and shall be the last to break off the struggle. It is evident that daybreak will end our resistance, for it is certain now that we cannot defeat them in battle. Not even the seeming impregnability of our fortress has sufficed to save us. Though we have food in abundance, ample supplies of arms, and more than enough of every other requisite, God himself has taken away all hope of survival. And I think it is God who has given us this night as a reward for our courage.

"In these moments left us, let us choose a noble end, preserving our freedom and maintaining our personal dignity. Since we must die, let it be by our own hands. It will be easier to bear. Let our wives die unabused, our children without knowledge of slavery, ourselves as free men. But first, let our possessions and the whole fortress go up in flames. It will be a bitter blow to the Romans to find us beyond their reach and nothing left for them to loot. Only let us spare some of our store of food. It will bear witness when we are dead that we perished not through want, but because we chose death rather than slavery."

When my father had finished speaking, it was clear that not everyone felt as he. In the din that ensued, those voices raised in rapturous support were countered by others whose pity for their beloved wives and children — and their abhorrence of such an end — showed in their tears and protests. "No. No!" some shouted. "It is to life we are dedicated — no matter what life it may be!"

Even to me the idea was repugnant. As a physician, I dedicated myself to saving life, not destroying it. My whole nature shuddered at the prospect.

Would I never again hear the trill of a bird? Feel the sun's warmth? Know the satisfaction of meaningful work? Enjoy the sweetness of friendship, family, and love? Was it to this end we had struggled so hard and so long?

Recognizing that those who had not flinched when they heard his proposal might now be influenced by other men's laments, my father, fired with passion, cried, "I thought I had the support of loyal followers in the struggle for freedom! Where are they now? Those who died in battle we may well congratulate; they died defending their freedom, not betraying it. But the masses

178

now under the thumb of Rome — who would not pity them? Some have been broken on the rack, or tortured to death at the stake or by the lash; some have been half-eaten by savage beasts and then kept alive to become their food a second time after providing amusement for their enemies. For those still alive, have pity; they pray and pray for the death that comes too slowly. Who would not hasten to die rather than share their fate?

"Is anyone too blind to see how furious the Romans will be if they find us alive in the morning? For have we not turned down their offers to spare us? Have we not fought off their legion these many months and murdered many of their bravest men? If they find us waiting, pity the young, whose bodies are strong enough to survive prolonged torture! Pity the not-so-young, whose old frames will break under their ill usage! A man will see his wife violently carried off; he will hear the voice of his child crying 'Father!' when his own hands are fettered. Come! While our hands are free and can hold a sword, let them do a noble service! Let us die unenslaved by our enemies and leave this world as free men in company with our wives and children. That is what our wives and children demand; that is what our laws command us to do — the opposite of what the Romans wish. Let us deny the enemy their hoped-for pleasure at our expense and leave them dumbfounded by our deaths and awed by our courage."

Much more my father said, and with such eloquence that at last all were convinced, and made haste to do the deed. As if possessed, they took lead of their friends and rushed to their dear ones, holding in their minds the vision of the agonies their families would suffer at the hands of the Romans.

My heart filled with a weight of tears as I pushed

179

through the crowd to my father to take my final farewell. Eleazar, head bowed, seemed lost in prayer. When he looked up, his eyes were blurred with tears. Wordlessly, we embraced. Then, still in silence, we turned toward the room where my mother would be.

My mother sat at a table that every Sabbath eve had served as the gathering place for our family. Before her, folded in a small, neat pile, were the clothes and linens of our household. Pots and cooking utensils, cosmetic jars and combs were carefully arranged, as though she had sat this last hour considering where each should be placed. Lying across her lap was a wooden stake made from a kitchen spoon, its bowl wound tight with cloth.

"Mother!" I rushed forward and fell on my knees before her, barely able to hold back the sobs that tore at my heart. She took my face in her hands and kissed my forehead. "I am glad we are together. It will not be so hard." She wiped tears from my cheeks and rose to meet my father. Taking his hands in hers, she drew him close, clinging to him for a moment. "I am ready now, Eleazar," she said with dignity and acceptance.

My father dipped the stake into a pot of oil at my mother's side and ignited the cloth from the small fire in the cooking stove. Then, holding hands, they stepped forward together and set our worldly goods afire. As we watched the flames consume all we owned, I knew that at that moment other families were doing the same in every room on Masada. And that men were smashing the jars of provisions in the storerooms and setting these afire, leaving only enough food to show the Romans that we perished not through want, but because we chose an honorable death.

"Now, I must ask a difficult thing of you, Berenice," my father said.

My mother turned an agonized face to him. "Yes, my husband?"

For a moment my father remained silent, as though gathering courage to speak. Then, in a very soft voice, he said, "Go to the cistern nearest the hanging palace and hide until this is over."

"What? What are you saying?" my mother cried out, backing away.

My father's voice was firm. "Berenice, this is no sudden whim. I have thought on it for some time. There must be someone to tell the Romans why we fought and why we died."

"Not I!" she cried, shaking her head. "Not I! I belong with you, with my people, my family. Eleazar, I beg you, not I!"

He shook his head sadly, and his voice trembled. "Dear wife, I wish with all my heart it were not so. But this is a sacrifice I can ask of no one else."

She began to sob. "No. No. Eleazer, do not ask this of me — please. I could not bear to live with everyone I care for lost to me. It is too cruel!"

My father took her hands and gazed into her eyes. "Do you not think I know what a terrible thing I ask? But someone must bear witness to our sacrifice. Who would the Romans believe other than a member of my family?"

"Simon! Ask Simon!"

"No, Berenice. Simon must help ben Ezra. It must be you."

For the first time in the long months that we had suffered under siege, my mother's strength seemed to leave her. She collapsed at my father's feet. He bent down and lifted her gently. His grief-stricken eyes studied her face as though memorizing every beloved feature.

"Go with her, Simon." He spoke with finality. "The

night grows short, and there is much to do before morning."

As I led my mother across the plateau to the cistern, I could see smoke and flames rising from the casemate rooms. Above the crackling of the fires I heard cries of pain and terror, and knew too well what they meant. In the end, not a man would fail to carry out his terrible resolve, each disposing of his loved ones by his own hand, knowing it was a lesser evil than awaited them on the morrow. And then they too would die at the hands of ten men, chosen by lot. At last, one poor soul would be charged to end the lives of those remaining — and then his own.

The doors to the cisterns had been locked. But this one, by my father's hand, had been left open. My mother seemed stunned, unaware of what was happening as I urged her down the dark steps to the level of the water. There, to my surprise, I found cowering in the darkness an old woman and several children. I had not the heart to argue with them or to urge them to join the others. I felt relief, in fact, that my mother would not face the Romans alone.

"Mother," I whispered sharply, trying to rouse her from her apathy. "Mother! I must go. Will you be all right?" She did not answer.

A lump formed in my throat as I withdrew my hand from hers. "Good-bye, mother dear," I whispered, kissing her wet cheek, then turning to leave.

"Simon!" she cried at last, calling my name again and again so that it echoed terrifyingly throughout the vast, nearly empty cistern. "Simon! Simon!" she begged as I closed the door to the cistern and rushed away.

I SIT HERE NOW, waiting, so horrified, so full of sorrow I can barely write. Only the fire crackling as it consumes

the medical supplies and furnishings of this poor room
breaks the silence. My thoughts go to Sara and Aram, to
mother and father. Around me lie the bodies of others I
have loved, those who gave purpose to my life: Ananus
ben Ezra and his wife; my beloved, Salome. All dead.
Dead by my hand.

And now it is my turn.

Will this journal, these scrolls survive the fire? And
the Romans? Will someone in some future time find these
words and understand how we lived and why we died
on Masada? I will never know.

Chapter XXV

*Masada, Kingdom of Judea
15 April, fourth year of
our Caesar Titus Flavius
Vespasianus*

Hail, Caesar:

On this day I occupied and claimed for Rome the fortress of Masada, the last Jewish stronghold in this kingdom to resist our forces.

Lest any question how a mere thousand Jews could hold off an entire Roman legion for seven months and three days, let him read these words with care.

Lest any challenge why such elaborate works as a three-mile circumvallation wall and a siege ramp of proportions never before attempted were necessary, let him read here all that happened on this day, that he may recognize the character of this enemy — the stubborn, single-minded passion of this adversary to remain free.

Following, I relate the circumstances of capture:

At dawn this morning, with twelve hundred men,

their commanders, and twelve centurions assembled before me, I gave the following address:

> Brave men of the Tenth Legion: Today we make the final assault on the Zealot stronghold. In a short time we will be standing upon the plateau we have worked so diligently and fought so valiantly to acquire. Not one of us will forget the cost of this achievement.
>
> It is only natural that you now look with relish for revenge, that you are eager for action, hungry for the spoils due you. Yet, I demand that you control these passions.
>
> I, Flavius Silva, your commander and governor of this conquered nation, declare that this day will mark the beginning of peace in this land. Judea has fallen; Masada, the last Jewish fortress, will soon be ours. Today we will take prisoners; only those who refuse to surrender will know our swords. There must be no more bloodshed. Mark me well!

In the faces before me, I read anger, disapproval, and resentment, but acceptance, too. I knew then how wise it had been to allow passions to cool overnight. I knew these men would exercise restraint, so that we could present our Caesar the last of the rebellious Jews.

I observed Marius. His eyes, cold and disapproving, studied me. His hand moved urgently, compulsively over the hilt of his sword. I can only believe it betrayed his determination to act as he saw fit.

The trumpets were sounded. The voices of the entire legion shattered the stillness with a great cry: "Charge!" Instantly, twelve hundred men, sun glinting off the metal of their armor, started up the ramp to the plateau of Masada.

Once through the rock wall that our battering ram had turned to rubble, we came upon the wood wall the Jews had hastily built, still smoldering. A crew of slaves pushed aside the charred remains with ease and cleared a passage through which we moved, twenty-five abreast, till we climbed at last beyond the wall and into the open.

The ground was littered with the debris of arrows, javelins, and stones. Fire seemed to be everywhere, yet not a Zealot did we see. Where were the defenders?

Our soldiers stood ready, swords drawn in the event of sudden attack. But the plateau remained curiously empty and silent. I heard only the whoosh of wind, caused by the fire sucking through the open doorways of the casemate wall.

As moments passed and still no human showed himself, I dispatched a squad of men to the nearest rampart rooms. They soon returned, looking perplexed; they could not access the burning apartments, and remarked on a peculiar odor, like that of burning flesh.

By this time we all spoke in whispers, for the silence seemed ominous. And we sought to hear any sound, other than the wind and crackling flames, that indicated the presence of the enemy.

"Perhaps they have massed at the buildings beyond," Marius offered, indicating with a nod the buildings to the north of where we stood.

"If so, we are close enough by now to have been struck by their arrows," I answered.

"Then where are they?" he demanded.

I clutched the stabbing pain in my belly as a terrible, improbable possibility came to mind.

"Hallo?" I shouted tentatively. There came no answer.

I gave the command, and a thousand voices shouted simultaneously, "Hallo!" As their cries faded, silence returned. I felt cold, chilled down to the marrow, certain now that the improbable had indeed come to pass.

As I ordered men to begin dousing the fires so we might enter the casemate rooms, my eye caught movement across the plateau. Coming toward me was a small knot of people.

For some reason, perhaps the desolation of the scene, I made no move to intercept the forlorn delegation. As I watched them approach, fire smoldered sullenly; wind blew fragments of burned cloth at my feet. At last I counted seven people: a very old woman, who picked her way cautiously through the rubble; five tattered and whimpering children; and a tall, thin woman in her middle years who strode purposefully toward me.

Something in the gaunt woman's bearing — the dignity and determination of her step, perhaps — held me and my men motionless. As she drew closer, her face a mask of controlled grief, no one moved or spoke.

I felt no pride or elation at our victory. Instead, I stood awkwardly silent, like an intruder at a funeral.

Suddenly, aware of how the children clung to her dress, impeding her progress, the woman paused to disengage them, stooping to embrace each briefly. Whatever she said to these children became clear, for they now paired up two and two, the tallest child falling back to take the hand of the old woman. Walking thus, the younger woman in the lead, they came at last to stand before me.

"I am Berenice, wife of Eleazar ben Ya'ir." She spoke in a voice devoid of expression.

Wife of the Jewish leader! "Where are the others?" I asked. Her face reflected a pain so raw, I felt my slightest show of compassion would destroy what little composure she had left. The woman shook her head; her lips

187

trembled, and her eyes, red and sunken, turned one last time to view the Zealot fortress before she spoke.

HERE I CONCLUDE this journal. The fortress Masada is now ours. Save for these few survivors, the defenders — nine hundred sixty prisoners I had hoped to take — are dead. This journal and the woman Berenice I send to you, my Caesar, that you may hear from her own lips the story of the Zealots of Masada.

Your servant,
Flavius Silva
Commander, Tenth Legion